The Ascen

Book 6

The King Revealed

Gary Richardson

First originally published by Gary Richardson 2024

ISBN 979-8-3507-2631-2 (Paperback)
ISBN 979-8-3507-2634-3 (eBook)

Printed in the United States of America

This last book in this series is dedicated to everyone who encouraged and supported me throughout the last years to bring this series to life.

Gary Richardson

Series Reminders

What follows is a summary reminder of all places, names, and other key identifiers which is coupled with a pronunciation guide in the previous books. Any places, names, or similar identifiers included in this book will have a similar pronunciation guide, so no fretting. Any new characters, places, or items introduced in this book will not appear in this list but will have an appropriate pronunciation guide in the book near its first appearance to avoid any potential spoilers.

Pronunciation guide:

Rishdel (Rish-del)   Skeel (Scale)

Corsallis (Cor-sol-is)   Triandal (Trin-dull)

Kirin (Kear-in)   Izu (Is-ew)

Bjiki (Bee-zee-key)   Arissa (Ah-riz-sa)

Mechii (Meh-chi)

Kaufmor (Cough-more)

Norsdin (Nor-sh-den)

Nefarion (Ne-fair-e-on)

Ailaire (El-air)

Ellias (El-i-us)

Raiken (Rye-ken)

Sagrim (Sag-rim)

Trylon (Try-lawn)

Rhorm (Roar-mm)

Macadre (Ma-cod-dre)

Riorik (Re-or-ick)

Cyrel (Sear-el)

Shadrack (Shad-rack)

Nordahs (Nor-duh-sh)

Nectana (Neck-ta-on-ah)

Heilstur (Hill-st-ur)

Aqutarios (Ah-k-tar-e-os)

Grue (Grew)

Kelig (Kale-ig)

Leza (Le-z-ah)

Baolba (Bowel-ba)

Derkar (Der-car)

Ami (Ah-me)

Ori (Or-ee)

U'gik (Ew-gick)

Veyron (Vay-ron)

Yorid (Your-id)

Bostic (Boss-tick)

Jayn (Jane)

Droth (Draw-th)

Brem (Brim)

Dylo (Die-low)

Theon (They-on)

Daldon (Dowl-don)

Kerros (Care-o-ss)

Draynard (Dre-nard)

Morthia (More-thigh-ah)

Fielboro (Fail-bore-o)

Asbin (As-bin)

Gromard (Grow-mard)

Tyleco (Tie-le-co)

Do'ricka (Door-ick-ah)

Argrip (Are-grip)

Perigrine (Pair-eh-grin)

Rakish (Rack-ish)

Tanion (Tan-ya-un)

Zox (like "socks" but with a z)

Arin (Are-in)

Neddit (Ned-it)

Valstrand (Veil-strand)

Pan (Pan)

Ammudien (Ah-mew-dee-in)

Aldiri (Al-dear-e)

Endol (In-doll)

Dhun (Dune)

Toby (Toe-be)

Kukri (coo-kree)

Deaijo (Day-hoe)

Wuffred (Woo-fred)

Brennan (Bren-in)

Dava (Day-va)

Klienheart (K-line-heart)

Via (Vie-ah)

Freca (Freh-ka)

Coway (Cow-way)

Aurochs (Or-awk-s)

Barbos (Bar-bo-s)

Alaricea (Ah-lar-eye-see-ah)

Magnus (Mag-n-us)

Algon (Al-gone)

Whilem (Will-um)

Shiron (Shear-on)

Feigh (Fay)

Villkir (V-ill-cur)

Bror (B-roar)

Turkin (Tur-kin)

Gary Richardson

Chapter 1

The united forces of Riorik and friends, along with the barbarian and

dwarven fighters, rushed onto the battlefield. The forces from the Narsdin

region were still making every effort to breach the defenses of Mechii, but

the new allies were determined to stop them. The gnomes had

successfully defended their home while Bror and Dhun did their part. The two barbarian scouts had disrupted the evil king's siege weapons that had relentlessly pounded the protective barrier spell covering the gnomish city.

The gnomes defending Mechii were slowly losing ground to the invaders, who prized quantity over quality as dozens and dozens of makeshift soldiers continued to try and push their way through the blockade. With their magic, the gnomes were easily able to dispatch individual enemies, but the raw number of enemies had begun to overwhelm their efforts. Magic spells required time to cast, and their magical defenses needed time to recharge. But both were hampered by the constant onslaught of enemies.

To buy time for their colleagues to prepare more spells, some of the gnomes even resorted to physical combat, something gnomes were neither known for nor skilled at.

The situation in Mechii was beginning to look desperate for the gradually retreating residents but they knew little of the battle's evolution outside of the city's gate.

Several dwarves armed with blunderbusses had stayed at the lone remaining catapult to operate the siege weapon, though they required the help of two barbarians to reach the components affixed above the dwarves' heads. They continued to load the catapult and launch its projectiles into the invading forces, being careful not to fire near their charging comrades. Some attacks were more successful than others, as some of the tossed boulders killed multiple opponents while others landed in unoccupied spaces, only managing to scatter some of their intended targets.

With each blow from his own weapon turned against them, the masked king grew more and more angry. He knew he had dispatched a group of soldiers to retake the giant machines but had been too distracted by the fight to enter Mechii to find out what happened to them. The king had no idea that his soldiers had been riddled with holes from the dwarves' new weapon, only that they had obviously failed at their task.

As he looked back over his shoulder at the catapult's location, the invading elf noticed a group larger than the force he'd dispatched was now headed in his direction. It was soon apparent to the skilled fighter that the shapes moving towards him were not his own forces but rather those opposed to his invasion.

The self-proclaimed king spun to face his encroaching attackers head on. With his eyes fully trained on the crowd, it didn't take long for him to recognize Riorik, who he'd fought at the oasis. The missing armor pieces that he'd failed to acquire then were now within his grasp once more, and the masked king was determined not to let them slip through his fingers a second time.

However, in his lust for the armor in Riorik's possession, the well-equipped invader failed to notice Kirin among those rushing towards his position. Unaware that his wizard had now joined forces with his enemies, the elven dictator ordered several nearby fighters to break from their assault

on Mechii and join him against the newest arrivals. The armored king and

his soldiers rushed forward to meet their attackers.

It didn't take long for the two groups to collide on the battlefield.

Ammudien and Kirin stayed towards the back of the fight, as with surgical

precision, they strategically cast various magical spells to defend their

friends or punish their enemies. The two magic users called upon almost

every spell in their collective repertoire. Small fireballs, acid splashes,

whirlwinds, quicksand, rock walls, and everything in between were used to

distract, deflect, defend, and dismay. At one point, Kirin even used a

teleport spell to fling a dark elf that almost reached Villkir's flank into the

path of the catapult's projectile. The careening rock splattered the

confused dark elf's body, sending a rain of blood, guts, and body parts

over the fighters as the catapult's missile came to a crashing halt on the

ground nearby.

The group's use of magic had not gone unnoticed though. It quickly drew the attention of the group's leader, who immediately recognized Kirin on the opposing side. There were few mages who were not of gnomish descent, and Kirin's robes had become familiar to the furious leader. "Traitor!" the vindictive king shouted as he pointed the glowing blade of his sword in Kirin's direction before using it to sever an attacking dwarf's arm from its body.

In fact, the invading elf had been so distracted by his greed and lust for Riorik's armor, combined with his rage at Kirin's betrayal, that he didn't notice just how poorly the fight around him had been unfolding for his side. The barbarians under Villkir's command had proven to be a very formidable force against the gnolls and orcs. The dwarves, with their small but stout bodies, could more than hold their own against their opponents. And then there was Riorik, Nordahs, and Rory fighting right in the thick of it all. The two Rangers and the veteran city guard each put their own skills on display as they dodged, deflected, and ducked to avoid the rather shabby attacks from their less skilled opposition, before stabbing, slicing, and eviscerating those same foes.

The fight was quickly turning against the masked king. Ammudien thought it might be worth calling for a surrender, considering their impending victory.

"It's over, Cyrel," the gnome called out to the Macadre's leader. "It's not too late to return to Rishdel and rejoin your family."

It was the first time in a long while that the invading king had heard the name Cyrel. He couldn't help but give a small grin at the sound of that name. For that brief moment, his anger subsided slightly as his thoughts drifted to a time when that name held meaning for him. But those memories quickly faded, and his rage not only returned but grew stronger as he looked at his sword's illuminated blade.

"There's no need to return to Rishdel. I will see that abomination of a village razed so completely that it will be only a distant memory, its name spoken only in whispers for fear that their fate will become the same as those who dwelled there," retorted the irritated elf.

His words confused Riorik. The young elf didn't understand why his father would harbor such ill will towards a town that once held him in such high regard. Cyrel Leafwalker was a hero to the Rangers who served with him and to all who lived under his protection prior to his going mad. Riorik could only assume that the madness that had taken his father's mind years before had somehow distorted his memories of home and turned him against those he once vowed to protect. Perhaps it was that same madness that drove him to kill his friend and ally, Shadrack Bladeleaf, Nordahs' father.

Riorik yearned to understand that madness but knew that now was not the time. The young Ranger was keenly aware of the danger that surrounded him and that if he wanted a chance to unravel this mystery more fully, then he would first have to survive. Riorik quickly pushed his thoughts and concerns to the back of his mind so that he could continue focusing on the fight in front of him. More and more of his father's troops seemed to appear.

In fact, several of the infantry near the back of the crowd that had gathered near Mechii's entrance noticed the second fight happening behind them. With the absence of absolute leadership or their leader's constant supervision and direction, many of the anxious soldiers ran to aid their king. But, while this put added pressure on Riorik and his allies, it also unintentionally relieved some of the pressure on the gnomes at the entrance.

#

At the gate, the gnomes soon noticed a decrease in the rate of soldiers pouring through. The invaders were still numerous, but as their entry pace slowed, the gnomes and their defenses were quickly able to take on a more offensive posture compared to their previous defensive stance. The gnome spellcasters wasted no time using various combinations of spells, like the wall of fire propelled by wind magic that Ammudien and Kirin had used against Lord Veyron and his troops, to expel what forces remained within the city's barrier.

After the city was secured and free of invaders, the gnomes took the fight out onto the battlefield with the others.

Fireballs, massive bolts of lightning, and powerful gusts of wind pummeled the retreating invaders as they desperately tried to dodge rock walls and barricades that sprung randomly out of the ground. The sheer amount of magic being unleashed on the open battlefield caused much disarray, confusion, and fear among those trying to get away. There were those who thought it wiser to attack the gnomes head on now that they were exposed in the open field, but they quickly came to regret that decision as they were swiftly targeted by several spells simultaneously.

When one dark elf tried to rush the gnomes, he was lifted and held in the air by a small tornado while being repeatedly struck with bolts of lightning. As the tornado abated, the elf was smashed under a rock with only an arm protruding from under the weighty stone.

Thinking an aerial attack might have better luck, a gnoll jumped from atop

the large rock that had just recently crushed the dark elf. But this attacker

didn't fare much better, as two more stones were materialized on

opposite sides of the flying beast and collided to squash the gnoll in mid-

air. The stones struck with such force that each of them broke into

thousands of shards that showered the area. Meanwhile, the gnoll was

compressed into a husk that sent blood spurting dozens of yards from

every orifice. Its intestines ruptured from the hairy creature's soft belly,

and the flattened foe drifted to the ground like a heavy piece of paper

falling through the air.

Chaos quickly spread as the troops continued to scatter. The cries and

screams from his troops eventually caught the attention of the elf who

had anointed himself as king of the northern region. Once more, the

armored king found his attention distracted from the fight at hand as he

looked at his disorganized and dysfunctional troops, desperately trying to

understand the source of their confusion. It didn't take the veteran elf long to recognize the threat of the gnomes now loose on the battlefield

and their impact on his troops.

The armored king immediately realized that this fight wasn't going to end

in his favor. To stay and fight would mean almost certain defeat,

something he was keen to avoid.

The gnomes had proven more difficult to conquer than he'd first expected,

thanks to their protective barrier spell. It created a dangerous bottleneck

for his ground troops while at the same time completely nullifying the

effects of his massive siege weapons.

And now, with the arrival of the barbarians, the dwarves, and Riorik's

group with their two pieces of the Ascension Armor, this was not a fight

the king could win. The only option was to retreat, regroup, and plan a

new approach if his invasion was still to succeed.

His plan of a stealthy invasion along the West coast had obviously failed,

and now with his presence known, it would be a much tougher fight.

Nevertheless, it was a fight he was still determined to have and to win. But first, he needed to free himself and his remaining troops from the immediate skirmish so that a better plan could be established.

"To me! To me!" he shouted to a group of orcs thundering by. They were attempting to flee the burning flames of a fire cone spell cast by a gnome mage.

Coming to a halt, the large beasts with their thick hide skin and brutish strength rallied around their leader, who had managed to separate himself from the fight raging on around him.

"We must not let these foul creatures capture our catapult. I'd rather see it reduced to splinters than in the hands of our enemy. Surround me and we'll make our way to it before killing our enemies there and destroying the catapult. Do you understand?" he asked of the slightly distracted and typically unintelligent bipeds.

Most of the group nodded, which was more than the armored king had expected, so he immediately put his plan into action before the dimwitted orcs could forget his orders. The orcs crowded around their leader, shielding him off from the various blades and projectiles still flying about on the battlefield. As a single unit, the ground-shaking force trundled off towards the catapult. The group pushed right through the middle of the fight that the elven king had just been in, dividing the fighters as the pack made its way across the field.

Riorik, Villkir, and the others, including their foes, stopped to stare in amazement as the formation barreled through them and continued towards the catapult.

The pause came to an end with the sound of the elf king's voice, rising from inside the circle of orcs.

"Retreat!" he yelled out to his remaining troops, who quickly began repeating the order for the others.

It didn't take long for the call to spread, and not a single soldier in the king's army thought twice about it. Seconds after hearing the command, the bulk of the remaining forces were already making their way back towards the city of Kern, eager to flee the magical vengeance of the gnomes.

Riorik and the others watched in disbelief as the scene turned from one of total war to that of insects scurrying from the light. Normally, winning armies would pursue those fleeing to take advantage of the retreating force's lack of rear guard. They could maximize the damage inflicted and claim a victory, but on this day, all involved were too weary from battle and too stunned by the sudden shift in the assault to think clearly. Instead, everyone watched as the northern forces fled the scene, except for the collection of orcs with their elven king at the center, who continued trudging towards the catapult.

#

The barbarians and dwarves still operating the catapult took notice of the approaching formation of orcs. The other forces had largely been too scattered or now were too far out of the catapult's range to warrant further action there, so there was little else to do but defend their position.

The barbarians, each outfitted with a large, two-handed battle-axe, readied their weapons and waited for the orcs to come within range. But the dwarves were not so patient. Many of those at the catapult grabbed their firearms, already locked and loaded. The lead dwarven marksmen issued orders to fire on the approaching orcs in groups of three so they could sustain a rate of fire that gave each group a chance to reload their weapons while being covered by the others.

The first trio of dwarves quickly stepped up, took aim on the advancing enemy, and unleashed the power of their weapons. A barrage of hot lead flew towards the orcs, and several of the small projectiles struck their intended targets. The orcs winced in pain as the hot balls of lead pierced their thick skins. The dwarven shooters had been mostly on target, but none succeeded in landing a lethal hit.

Those three dwarves quickly retreated behind the next three who stepped up and fired on the orcs. More balls of super-heated lead found their mark, pelting the orcs all over their massive bodies. But again, no orc was felled by the assault as they got closer and closer to the now nervous dwarves.

The next three took their positions and fired another barrage in the direction of the orcs. This time, however, their aim was less accurate than the first two squads. The hand cannons were already difficult to aim and made harder by the massive amount of smoke each blunderbuss put out, clouding the battlefield. Several of the projectiles missed their targets completely, with some of the errant shots even striking one of the barbarians near Villkir and Riorik's group, sending the elf and his friends scrambling for cover.

As the smoke cleared, partly with the help of a quick wind spell cast by Kirin, the dwarves could see the efforts of their work. An orc from the formation's left side had fallen. Their shots had not been entirely on target, but some did manage to find that orc. Encouraged, the first trio of

dwarves were ready to fire again and wasted no time in sending another

round of lead towards the orcs who had now almost reached their

position.

The two remaining orcs at the front of the formation took several more

hits before succumbing to their wounds, leaving the armored king

exposed. His frontline was downed by the blunderbusses, but there were

still nearly half a dozen orcs with him, headed towards the dwarves. Now

was not the time to stop firing, and they knew it.

With the cycle renewed, the next trio of shooters stepped up and fired on

the group of foes. Another orc fell, having taken a shot directly in the eye

and another in its throat. But, much to the amazement of the dwarves,

several of their projectiles simply bounced off the group's leader and his

glowing breastplate. Surprised but undeterred, the dwarves swapped

positions again, and another volley was fired in his direction. This time two more orcs fell, but again, the king's armor deflected the blasts as if they were no more than rocks thrown by children.

The dwarves knew about the armor but not that their opponent possessed two pieces of it. The faint blue glow should've given it away, but stories of the armor were largely considered fables and not a matter of truth. The dwarves were unprepared for what they were seeing. Though they didn't understand how the king could withstand the impact from their weapons, the dwarves were no less intent on using them as they prepared to fire the next round.

Again, the battlefield was covered in smoke, so the dwarves had little choice but to wait for the smoke to clear. Kirin prepared another spell to help, but that help would come too late for the dwarves.

Kirin managed to sweep the smoke aside just in time for the dwarven shooters to be confronted with their enemy in close combat. The armored king and the lone remaining orc emerged from the smoke to attack the surprised group. The orc focused on the two barbarians while the masked king took on the dwarves.

One orc versus two barbarians was not a fight in the orc's favor and didn't last long. Equipped with only a massive wooden club, the orc swung his hefty weapon at the nearest barbarian, who deftly blocked the attack. Using the blade of his battleaxe, the barbarian smartly caught the orc's wooden weapon, the force of the orc's swing impaling the club firmly onto the axe head, merging the two weapons. The orc struggled to free his weapon from the barbarian's axe while the barbarian held firm to the handle, working against the orc's efforts in order to delay the beast.

As the distracted orc fought to retrieve his weapon, the other barbarian cautiously took up position behind the simple-minded oaf. The stout barbarian tightened his grip on his axe's handle and raised the powerful weapon high above his head. Taking aim at the distracted orc's back, the barbarian lunged forward and brought the blade down with all the force he could bring to bear. A squishing sound quickly followed by a loud snap could be heard as the battleaxe buried itself deep in the orc's flesh, slicing right through the beast's spine in the process.

The struggling orc immediately went stiff as the blow severed its spine. The beast could no longer move. Frozen in place, held upright by its grip on the club and the axe now wedged in its back, the orc could do nothing as the life slowly drained from its body. As the orc grew weak, the muscles in its hands relaxed, freeing the club from its grip. It teetered forward, forcing the barbarian behind it to let go of the battleaxe still embedded in the beast's back. Orc and axe both fell forward as the last gasp of life escaped from the its open mouth.

Meanwhile, the dwarves had their hands full with the skilled and well-equipped elven leader. One dwarf thought to try firing at close quarters to see if his gun would have more effect at a closer range, but as he took aim, the masked invader used his glowing sword to strike the blunderbuss's frame. The bright blade easily sliced through the weapon's metal and wood construction, like a blade through water.

Gary Richardson

The bisected firearm fell to the ground, and the blow also severed the dwarf's fingers where they'd been holding the stock. It would've taken the dwarf's other arm too had he not jerked it away at the last second. The injured dwarf cried out in pain as he held the bloodied remains of his hand up in front of his face, staring at it in disbelief. His moment of disbelief was brief, however, as his attacker took the opportunity to land an uncontested blow.

This time, the elf's sword gracefully and without hesitation slid across the dwarf's midsection, just below his ribs. The dwarf stood paralyzed by the sudden attack. He blinked, a stunned expression on his face. His mouth still hung open from his previous cries of pain, but now, no sound was emitted. The cold, undisturbed elf casually walked toward the dwarf and ever so slightly nudged his head. The dwarf's top half separated from his bottom half, sliding to the ground in a pool of viscera and blood.

The other dwarves jumped back from the horrible sight and instinctively fired their weapons at the aggressor. Again, their bullets merely bounced off the armor as the elf used his vambraces to shield his more vulnerable head. Luckily for him, the dwarves always aimed for the body and never the legs, allowing the king's mystical armor to absorb the damage that might otherwise have proven lethal.

Outraged by the continued annoyances of the dwarves and their weapons, the elven invader decided it was time for him to retreat and rejoin his forces at their base camp in Kern.

The king turned and made his way the last few feet to the final remaining catapult. One of the barbarians attempted to stop him, but using the strength granted to him from the breastplate, the bearer of Trylon's breastplate swatted away the barbarian as one would an insect, sending him tumbling backward across the ground.

With no other obstructions, the King of Narsdin reached the catapult and with a single swing of his blade, he split the main support of the massive construction. A normal blade would not have been able to cleave through such a large, thick piece of timber, but Raiken's sword was made from heavenly Dragon Steel ore and had no problem slicing cleanly through the material, It took no damage, no dulling of the blade's razor-sharp edge. The empty battlefield was filled with the sounds of creaking and cracking as the catapult's superstructure struggled to stay upright with its main support beam now split in two. The ropes stretched and eventually gave way. They snapped, putting more pressure on the wooden structure and the simple wooden pegs used to lock the various pieces together. In a few quick seconds, the catapult crumbled, tumbling in the direction of the dwarves and barbarians who'd failed to defend it.

The collapsing, over-sized weapon sent the defenders scurrying in every direction, desperate to avoid being trapped under the falling logs that would surely crush anyone unfortunate enough to be caught under them. In the chaos he'd created, the elf king took his chance to escape unnoticed. He fled to northward, the same direction his troops had fled only moments before. The cape draped across his shoulders helped to obscure the breastplate's glow from those behind him, and he sheathed his sword to minimize the amount of light his armor gave off, not wanting to give away his position.

The fight for Mechii was now over, but what would happen next, nobody knew.

Chapter 2

By the time Riorik and the others gathered near the gate, the gnomes of

Mechii had already started celebrating their successful defense of the city.

Ammudien walked alone in front of the others, and the group was careful

not to do anything that might be construed as aggressive. Considering

what had just transpired, he made his presence obvious to the city's

defenders, who might still be wary of outsiders.

"Friend or foe?" a gnome called out as the group approached, bringing the celebration to an immediate halt.

"Friend," Ammudien quickly answered. "It is I, Ammudien of the House Flickerspell. I have returned from my self-imposed exile and bring with me friends to help combat this newly revealed enemy."

"And how can we be so certain that these 'friends' of yours can be trusted and that you are not under their control?" the cautious gnome asked.

"Some of these fine folks have fought alongside me against this enemy once before, and the others aided us in your defense just now," Ammudien Flickerspell replied confidently.

"No such aid was witnessed here," huffed the gnome, still not entirely sure of Ammudien's assertions.

"I can certainly believe that," Ammudien calmly responded. "It looked as if you all had your fill of enemies here, trying to break through the barrier that has shielded our great city for generations. Mounting such a defense against that mob was no small feat and would surely have kept your focus.

But, regardless of what you may or may not have seen, I remain steadfast in my knowledge that these folks are not your enemy and have come to help."

Murmurs echoed through the group of gnomes as they contemplated Ammudien's words. There were those among the gnomes who remained reluctant to welcome outsiders into their ranks. Eventually, those who acknowledged Ammudien's family's house, which apparently held some sway among the gnomes, outnumbered those who resisted his claims, and the gnomes approached to greet their new comrades in war.

As the gnomes discussed the battle with their new allies, an elderly gnome took notice of Riorik's radiant greaves. The old gnome with his long, white beard politely pulled Riorik away from the others so they could speak a bit more privately.

"Tell me, young elf, how did you come to possess such an odd garment?" the gnome asked Riorik.

Riorik was unsure how to answer the question. He wondered if the gnome was testing him or if the gnome simply thought the armor's appearance to be odd. Riorik settled on feigning ignorance, hoping the gnome would not know of the armor's power and legacy.

"What? These old things?" Riorik started as he tried to casually dismiss the armor's importance. "This is just standard gear given to all Rangers of my rank." Riorik hoped his lie would be enough to fool the inquisitive gnome.

The gnome just chuckled at Riorik's answer.

"Don't fret, young one. If you truly have the blessing from a member of the House Flickerspell, then you're among friends here. There's no reason to lie."

Although the gnome hadn't believed such a stupid lie, Riorik was still wasn't inclined to reveal the truth so easily.

"I apologize for my poor attempt at deceit," Riorik apologized to the gnome. "Truth be told, I picked these up in the markets of Tyleco. Rangers usually only wear leather, but I wanted something more substantial protecting me."

The gnome simply chuckled again at Riorik's latest lie.

"How do you expect us to be allies if we can't be honest with one another?" the gnome asked Riorik. "I know what it is that you wear. Those were made for your ancestor Ailaire many years before your birth. That is more than just mere armor. You and I both know this to be true, so there's no reason to continue this farce with me."

The gnome's words made it plain to Riorik that his ruse had not worked. He was left with no choice but to come clean with the small gnome. But the elf opted to only tell the gnome about the greaves, since that was all he'd asked about. The shield of Sagrim would remain Riorik's secret—for now.

Riorik recounted the story of how he, Ammudien, Nordahs, Asbin, and Wuffred found the tomb under the crumbling tower outside of Tyleco. The young elf described their fight with the bandits that surrounded the tower, the poison blade that nearly ended his quest, and Asbin's mixture, which eventually healed him. Riorik even told the old gnome about confronting the masked elf at the oasis, leading to Wuffred's death, but he was careful to leave out any mention of Sagrim's shield and the part it played in that fight.

"That's some adventure that you and your friends have been on from the sounds of it," the elderly gnome said once Riorik finished his story. "You know, many have searched their entire lives for that armor only to die having never laid eyes on it. To possess it is something most would think impossible, but it should go without saying that there are undoubtedly those out there who would wish to take those from you—without hesitation, and with force if necessary. I would caution you to only wear them in times of great need and keep them hidden from sight when speaking to strangers. You never know what greed and dark ambitions lurk in the hearts of others. It would not be wise to advertise your prize so openly."

Riorik instantly understood the gnome's warning and quickly worked to remove the unusually pliable armor before stuffing it once more deep into the depths of his pack. Satisfied that the greaves were safely hidden away, the gnome led Riorik back to the group to rejoin the celebration. However, their meeting with the gnomes would have to conclude soon. There were still far more pressing matters at hand.

#

The army which had marched from Macadre to Mechii in strict formation now hurried to Kern in disorder, bordering on chaos. Those that hadn't been killed in the failed assaults on Mechii and Rhorm ran from the battlefield. There were no thoughts of rank, honor, or respect among the routed. Only self-preservation. Even if someone had thought to try to gain control of the chaos, nobody knew who had perished and who had not, so the hierarchy of command had collapsed. None among them knew who the highest-ranking survivor was, which created a power vacuum because nobody knew who was authorized to command who. All any of them knew was that their supreme leader had ordered a full retreat to Kern.

The fleeing army scrambled down the same road back to Kern that they'd marched on to assault Mechii. It was the only road the invaders knew. What they didn't know was who else was on that same road, headed toward them.

Several minutes after fleeing the fight at Mechii, the retreating forces of Narsdin came face to face with the mounted soldiers of Tyleco under Lord Veyron's command.

The armored and decorated horses of Tyleco slid to a stop. Their riders were confused by the sight of so many unfamiliar groups before them. The soldiers of Tyleco had seen gnolls before, some even recently, but the dark elves, orcs, and trolls were totally foreign to the riders, who had little knowledge of life beyond the walls of Tyleco. All they had been taught was that under Lord Veyron's rule, Tyleco stood as a beacon of justice against the unfriendly forces outside its walls.

However, Lord Veyron was not confused at the sight of the fleeing forces of Narsdin. Being a human of noble birth, his upbringing had included an education that most of his subjects were not privy to, so he was able to recognize the terrible figures standing across from him for what they were, a horde of uncivilized and unfriendly inhabitants from the northernmost region, sworn enemies of all the things Tyleco was supposed to stand for. Even if these days Tyleco's image was only used to support Lord Veyron's claim to rulership over all of the humans in Corsallis.

Regardless of Tyleco's current political standing, Lord Veyron knew that whoever controlled this horde had not sent them here in the name of peace and that their very proximity to Tyleco put his life in grave danger. He knew that he now had to choose between running away like a coward or fighting like a warrior and a king. Lord Veyron, in his aspirations to be king, opted for the latter. He felt running away would show weakness, which might cost him support for his bid for the throne. However, if he knocked back this horde, then it could win him favor from those who had opposed him previously, perhaps even enough to tip the scales in his favor to finally be crowned.

Lord Veyron thrust his sword above his head and slowly lowered it in the direction of the stunned horde.

"Charge!" Lord Veyron yelled as he spurred his mount into battle.

The retreating horde was still too exhausted and terrified from their last battle to fight. As the humans and their horses charged, the entire horde broke in unison and and ran back down the road toward Mechii.

Lord Veyron and his men pursued.

It didn't take long for the horde to encounter their master, still headed towards Kern.

"What is the meaning of this?" the masked elf asked angrily. "I ordered you to retreat to Kern. Why are going in the opposite direction?"

A winded dark elf spoke up first.

"Humans on horses have blocked our path and pursue us even as we speak."

This was more than the armored king could handle. Not only had his plans for a quick and quiet invasion failed, but now it would seem that his stronghold in the region was lost to him. Now that the humans were approaching, and the gnomes and dwarves would likely follow soon, there was little time to weigh his options and come up with a new plan. The leader of all Narsdin would have to improvise and fast.

"Go west," he immediately ordered. "Make for the town of Brennan. We may be able to find refuge among the scoundrels that dwell there, but if nothing else, perhaps we can storm their city gates and secure ourselves protection while we regroup."

The horde didn't hesitate. They turned and continued fleeing to the west. Brennan was a ways away, and they had no choice but to continue running from the humans. But they didn't run fast enough. The speedy horses from Tyleco caught up with the retreating horde. Many of the riders were equipped with lances that allowed them to stab and impale their targets from a safe distance. The only saving grace for the retreating horde was that the jarring motion of the galloping horses made the riders less than steady with their aim. Many attempts missed their targets outright while others only managed glancing blows that resulted in simple flesh wounds. The armored elven leader wasted no time in making his way through his troops to face the Tyleco cavalry threatening what remained of his conquest.

One rider quickly zeroed in on the elf with the glowing armor that now stood motionless in the middle of the road. The rider turned his horse to face his target. He spurred his horse with his armor-clad heels while he whipped the horse's sides with his long leather reins, eager to get all of the power and speed he could from his mount. The horse raced towards the still motionless figure as the Tyleco guard carefully lowered his lance and took aim.

The masked elf watched as the horse and rider approached. He rose his fist and banged on his chest as if to dare the rider to strike at the illuminated armor.

The elf's taunt worked as the rider dropped the tip of his lance the few inches to aim at the bigger target, an almost guaranteed hit.

The elf remained unmoved by the threat racing towards him. The rider smiled gleefully at what he expected to be an easy kill. But the reality of what would unfolded was nothing like what the young human had anticipated.

The wooden weapon's metallic tip did not penetrate the elf's armor. Instead, the lance began to crumble against the impenetrable surface of the armor under the driving force of the horse's gallop. The armored elf was pushed back along the dirt road a few feet before he braced himself against a nearby rock. This put even more pressure on the already strained weapon.

The weapon's tipped snapped off as the wooden lance cracked and splintered under the pressure. Finally, the lance burst apart, showering the area with thousands of splintered shards of wood. The explosive force of the weapon's disintegration knocked its wielder off-balance, causing the rider to fall from his precarious position atop the horse.

The saddle offered no resistance to counter the rider's fall as it was only designed to provide a cushion and stirrups to the rider. So when the rider became dislodged, the saddle was no help. He was knocked from his mount and landed with a hard thud on the ground below. The thin metal helm that he wore offered little protection as his head slammed into the ground. The rider was instantly knocked unconscious, but for those watching, they all assumed the blow had killed him.

The unfolding scene caused the other riders of Tyleco to panic. Chaos erupted, and the riders scattered. Their lances were obsolete against such armor, that much was obvious to them all. Each of the riders carried swords and other weapons of war, but no one wanted to approach the armored elf still defiantly standing in the road and taunting them.

Lord Veyron was forced to pull his troops back. Having seen Sagrim's shield in his talks with Ammudien and Rory before, he instantly recognized his opponents glowing breastplate as another piece of the legendary armor.

It was now obvious to Lord Veyron that Ammudien and Rory's story about the wicked invader from the North was true and that his possession of at least one piece of the Ascension Armor made him a very dangerous and credible threat.

Lord Veyron had no choice but to abandon his pursuit of Ammudien and his previous captain of the guard in exchange for rallying the full might of his troops in order to defeat this new foe. A foe that threatened not only his claim to the throne but his very existence.

#

"So, the House of Flickerspell?" Nordahs said to Ammudien inquisitively.

"Are you some kind of gnomish royalty or something?"

"No, nothing like that," Ammudien calmly answered. "The gnomes of Mechii have no royal social structure as the humans do. No, we are more like you elves in that our city is governed by various boards, committees, and councils."

"And the Flickerspell family leads many of those boards, committees, and councils?" Nordahs asked in response to Ammudien's explanation.

"The Flickerspell family was among the first who settled here and formed what would eventually become Mechii. Over the years, there have been many of my family line who have held prominent and influential positions throughout the city. I, however, am not one of those gnomes, but my family name does still encourage others to behave positively towards me in hopes of gaining my family's support or vote on various matters. It's quite sickening honestly, but there are times that it does come in handy."

"So, it's like you are royalty then. Just admit it," Nordahs jokingly urged his smaller friend.

Ammudien smiled and gave a subtle nod at his friend's joke before Rory interrupted the pair.

"Why are we still standing around here talking?" Rory asked rhetorically. "Our enemy is weakened and in retreat. Now's not the time to talk or celebrate but to vanquish our foe and claim real victory."

The elf and gnome could hear the frustration in the human's voice. They both agreed with his sentiment, but there was little they could do to hurry the awkward alliance between the gnomes, dwarves, and barbarians now taking place.

These were three groups of people who'd interacted very little with one another for generations but were now united against a common enemy. Breaking down the social barriers that had built up over the years wasn't something that could happen in an instant, and the trio of friends watched as Riorik moved between groups, acting as a mediator when arguments inevitably broke out. They'd tried to help him but found that they lacked the charisma and skillful political tongue that Riorik seemed to possess. He could diffuse and de-escalate any situation much better than they could. All they could do was sit back, watch, and be ready to intervene if an argument devolved into a brawl, which happened more than once between the barbarians and dwarves, who often argued over who was stronger or who were the better fighters.

In fact, it was during one of these dust-ups that the trio missed seeing the old, grumpy dwarf leader grab Riorik by the arm and pull the young elf off to the side for a private conversation.

This was the second time in the span of several minutes that Riorik had been pulled aside by someone. He was beginning to think he'd have to have these one-on-one chats with everyone here before they could leave. Riorik was just as eager as the others to continue their pursuit, but he knew that they would need the help of all those gathered here to be victorious, so he tried to be amenable to their needs. And now, it seemed that another discreet chat was needed.

"Now that we have a few minutes alone, I would like to know more about this Wuffred character," the grumpy dwarf said, wasting no time with pleasantries or otherwise.

Riorik was grateful for the dwarf's bluntness but still questioned the timing of such a conversation.

"Are you sure now is the best time to discuss this?" Riorik questioned. "Do you not think we should chase after the retreating enemy instead?"

The grumpy dwarf just huffed at Riorik's questions.

"Listen here, lad," the dwarf started, "that foe isn't going anywhere. There's a reason for his coming here, and the fact that he tried to ambush not only us dwarves but also the gnomes can only mean that he fears an all-out war. He knows our forces are too many and his are too few to engage us all together. Let 'im run away and lick his wounds for tonight because come tomorrow, the united forces you see gathering before you will defeat his cowardly ambitions."

The dwarf's confidence did little to assuage Riorik's concerns. After all, Riorik knew about the pieces of the Ascension Armor in his father's possession, and that alone made him a force to be reckoned with.

With the armor, he was unlike anything or anyone ever confronted across any battlefield throughout time. Nonetheless, it was apparent to Riorik that there was little chance he could convince the dwarf otherwise. Stuck there for the foreseeable future, Riorik had no other option but to engage in the dwarf's desired topic of discussion—Wuffred.

"So, what can I tell you about Wuffred?" Riorik asked with a tinge of defeat in his voice.

"First, I want to know what kind of person he was. You said he died in battle, right? Well, what happened?"

Riorik wanted to choose his words very carefully. The dwarf had not made mention of Wuffred's berserker heritage. Riorik didn't know if Asbin had told anyone about Wuffred's condition. He didn't want to be the one to spill those beans, knowing that to do so might jeopardize both Asbin's and the baby's safety if the dwarves of Rhorm reacted to berserkers the same way Riorik's people had reacted to Wuffred.

Instead, Riorik opted to speak about Wuffred's bravery and strength, but he chose to do so in a way that hid the human's less desirable heritage.

"Wuffred was abandoned as a child and came to live with the elves," Riorik started, deciding to fib about Wuffred's true origins to prevent any questions or concerns the dwarf may have about a human living among the elves.

"The Rangers who found him thought his family was killed by animals," Riorik added. "Regardless, Wuffred was trained as a Ranger alongside myself and my friend Nordahs."

Riorik paused for a moment to point out Nordahs to the dwarf.

"Anyways, the three of us were sent out to search for my missing father, who was also a high-ranking Ranger."

Another small, harmless lie that Riorik felt gave their quest validity while further helping to conceal Wuffred's true reason for leaving Rishdel.

"Our search drew us into multiple encounters with gnolls and orcs, who had apparently been sent as advance scouts in preparation for the invasion you all helped repel. In those fights, Wuffred fought bravely, suffering many injuries that Asbin thankfully applied her healing techniques on. Without her, he would've surely been lost long before that fateful day at the oasis."

"The oasis?" the dwarf asked curiously at this.

"Yes, Asbin left to return to Rhorm as we prepared to leave Tyleco. We parted ways with her there, and our path led us to a small oasis North of Kern. It was there that we confronted the army's leader for the first time. He was without his army, and we assumed he had ridden ahead for some reason or another, but regardless, he was alone when our paths crossed."

Again, Riorik opted to omit Kirin's presence at the oasis in support of their shared enemy. Obviously, Riorik refused to identify that enemy as his father.

"We must've caught him by surprise because he immediately attacked us. He was stronger than any of us. Wuffred and I fought against him while Nordahs and Ammudien, the gnome just over there," Riorik added as he pointed out the short mage to the dwarf, "stood watch at the perimeter. The fight did not go our way. My attacks were largely unsuccessful, but Wuffred was able to land a few good shots that at least caused our opponent to bleed, so we learned he can be hurt.

"But, in the end, I was knocked to the ground and defenseless. Our foe approached with every intention of killing me when Wuffred came to my rescue again. The two tussled in the sand before the dark foe speared Wuffred through the chest with a sword. There was little Wuffred could have done to dodge or block the attack, but it gave me enough time to escape my certain death.

"We hurried back to Tyleco and Rishdel to warn the others of the impending invasion. That's when we sent word to Rhorm and many of the other towns."

The dwarf slowly nodded his head as Riorik's story ended but said nothing. He was taking in all that Riorik had to say, giving serious thought to what to say next. The two stood in silence for several seconds while the dwarf contemplated his next question, and when he asked it, it was a tough one for Riorik to answer.

"And how was it that during all this, my daughter had time to become romantically involved with this Wuffred?"

The question by itself was difficult enough to answer, but the sudden discovery that the grumpy dwarf was Asbin's father only made things worse.

"Well, I'm not sure, sir," was all Riorik was able to manage at first. "The two spent quite a lot of time together after she treated Wuffred's wounds. At that time, we hadn't yet added Ammudien to our party, so Nordahs and

I were responsible for protecting and providing for her and Wuffred while she put her tradecraft to use. I assume while Nordahs and I were distracted by our responsibilities that a bond formed between them. And I'll be honest, my focus was on finding my father, leaving plenty of opportunities for something to happen under my nose but still go unnoticed."

Riorik stopped there but then quickly thought of something more to add.

"But," he said quickly before Asbin's father could say anything, "I saw Wuffred put Asbin's safety before his own on more than one occasion. The feelings he had for her were genuine, and I think her feelings matched his. The idea of her being pregnant was a surprise to him just as much as the rest of us," Asbin continued, "but at no point after she had revealed her condition did his affection for her diminish. If anything, it only grew."

Content that he'd painted Wuffred in a positive light, Riorik decided it was time to stop talking before his words betrayed him and he said something that he might later regret.

"I see," Asbin's father casually replied. "And have you sent word to my daughter about Wuffred's end?"

This was the question that Riorik had dreaded. He had intentionally left out any details about Wuffred's death in his message to Rhorm. He wanted to tell Asbin what happened in person instead. But now, he had to explain that decision to probably the toughest critic possible—her father.

"No. No, sir," Riorik said with a slight stutter. Anxiety began filling his body. "I wanted to tell her face-to-face and be there for her if she needed anything after hearing what I assume will be devastating news. I felt it too personal a subject to be conveyed by messenger bird."

The dwarf nodded in agreement with Riorik's reasoning.

"That's a noble thought, young one," the dwarf replied. "I think I would be more upset had you sent such news to my pregnant daughter via bird. Her emotions run amok in her delicate condition, and I fear that painful news delivered in such an impersonal manner would cause her too great a strain. I only fear that if you are not more careful, you will not be alive at the end of all this to tell her yourself."

"Speaking of her condition, how is she doing? I assume by your words that the baby has not come yet. How much longer does she have?"

It warmed the dwarf's heart to hear Riorik ask about his daughter's condition. Her father could hear his sincere concern for Asbin and the baby in Riorik's voice. It reinforced Asbin's assurances that Riorik's true nature lacked any prejudice against those of different races.

"She is well, thank you for asking," her father gladly answered. "The priestess rests in the family home but remains very pregnant. Dwarven pregnancies last for at least ten new moons or roughly three-hundred days. She tells me that during your adventures together you found the healing fountain, and through its powers, it not only healed your wounds but accelerated her condition. Nobody is really sure just how much longer she has before the baby comes, but we all assume it will be soon. Perhaps when we have this business with this invader behind us, you can be there when the child comes."

It was the first time the dwarf hadn't spoken to Riorik with his usual gruff, grumpy tone. Maybe Riorik's answers and concerns had won over the worried father, he thought to himself. And they had. Asbin's father felt more at peace knowing that his daughter had been respected, loved, and cared for in her time with the group. But he was now saddened by the fact that he would have to return to Rhorm without Wuffred and look into his daughter's eyes as he revealed the truth to her. No father wants to see their children hurt, but unlike physical injuries, emotional ones take longer to mend, and there's little that anyone can do, even a father.

It took a moment to sink in, but eventually, Riorik realized that the dwarf had referred to Asbin as a priestess, something she hadn't shared with the group before.

"Priestess?" Riorik suddenly asked, obviously confused. "She said she came from a family of smiths that created the legendary armor and that she had been charged with finding the lost pieces."

"Well, that is true," the dwarf answered. "Asbin does come from a family of smiths. The Firehammer family has been among the elite smiths of Rhorm for generations, passing the crafting skills from father to son in each new generation. That tradition came to an end with Asbin's lot. I have failed to produce a male heir but was blessed with Asbin. Her magical attunement is above average among dwarves, which made her a perfect candidate to join the healers, where she was promoted to priestess. She was well on her way to becoming the High Priestess before she volunteered to seek the armor, which our family has indeed been searching for over the many years since our ancestors created it."

"What do you mean volunteered? She said she was the only suitable candidate, so it was her obligation to seek the armor. You make it sound as if she had a choice where she claimed to have none," Riorik said, still confused by the recent news regarding Asbin's true background.

"Of course she had a choice. She's not my only child, just the oldest. Her younger sister, Arala[1], could just as easily have searched for the armor. But Asbin, being the protective sibling she is, felt the search would be too dangerous for her baby sister and volunteered to take Arala's place. We argued with Asbin that her place was at the temple, but she's just as hard-headed as I am and wouldn't listen to reason. We knew if we tried to forbid her from going that she would just go anyway, so we simply let her go. Once Asbin's mind is made up about something, there is no changing it."

The part about being stubborn certainly sounded like Asbin to Riorik, but he was still in shock at learning that Asbin was really a priestess of the dwarven temple. Now it made sense to the young elf that she knew about the healing fountain and how to cure the bandit's poison. Asbin was more

---

[1] Pronounced "Uh-rah-la"

than a simple healer. She may have come from a family of elite smiths, but Asbin was considered among the elite of Dwarvish clerics.

"Come now," Asbin's father said to Riorik as he gave the elf a firm pat on the back. "Let's see if we can't get these other fools moving finally. I mean, if we want to return to Rhorm in time to see the baby being born, we can't very well stand around here any longer."

The dwarf's attitude had taken a complete turnabout. Riorik was left in amazement at the sudden change but didn't hesitate to jump at the dwarf's offer to help continue the pursuit.

Chapter 3

Having thwarted the Tyleco cavalry, the invading king rejoined the remnants of his army. He led them west across the plains towards the bandit town of Brennan. There was no question that the others would be hot on their heels in pursuit, so there was great uncertainty among the marching troops about whether they'd even reach Brennan without another fight.

The armored leader led the way in utter silence. The unexpected loss of his siege weapons and the devastating power of the dwarven blunderbusses had completely changed the landscape of the conflict. The aged elf was quick to acknowledge that no amount of gear or armor, besides his own, could withstand the firepower now held in the hands of dozens of dwarves. And without his siege weapons to strike from afar, the king's troops would have little choice but to move within the hand cannons' range to attack the dwarves with their puny-by-comparison bows and arrows.

This presented a formidable challenge for the invader. Several of his troops remained at Kern, but his path to the city had been blocked by Lord Veyron. He now marched towards Brennan after having suffered far greater losses at Mechii and Rhorm than expected. If the humans there resisted his offer, he was unsure whether he had enough troops to force Brennan into cooperation.

But even more worrying was the fact that now there was no option to retreat to Macadre. The northern forces were now trapped between the very people and cities he intended to conquer. The gnomes and dwarves would be coming from the east and south, limiting his movement options in those directions. Tyleco and Lord Veyron's army stood north of his current position, blocking any attempts at a direct retreat to the Narsdin region. Like Baolba before him, the horde's leader had no choice but to push on to the West.

Thankfully, the gnomes, dwarves, and barbarians weren't as keen to chase them as he'd feared, and Lord Veyron's mounted troops had hurried back to Tyleco to secure more men. This left the king's befuddled and exhausted horde in peace for their journey towards Brennan, giving them a much-needed break to regain their wits, strength, and will to carry on. Through the dark of night, the massive group of fighters, brawlers, mercenaries, and soldiers marched on.

The silhouette of Brennan could be seen on the horizon as the day's first light reached the horde. It was both a curse and a blessing to see the city so near. Brennan's appearance signaled the near end of their hike but also the potential start of another battle, one with much fewer troops than they'd expected to have for the coming confrontation. Regardless, the horde continued forward, hoping to find asylum rather than conflict. They would have their answer in just a few short hours—the time needed for them to cover the remaining distance to the city's gates.

The self-appointed king spent that time thinking of how he planned to approach the city's leaders to gain their support. A show of force was always a good option in his mind, but given his army's recent losses, he didn't want to invite further conflict or loss unless necessary. He contemplated subterfuge, perhaps waiting until nightfall and sending in some of his stealthier fighters with orders to assassinate people of high standing in the city. He could usurp their power and win the city in the absence of any authority. But no sooner had the idea had crossed his mind than he immediately realized it would take too long and require time he did not have.

And then it hit him.

Bribery was a tried and true method, one that that had found success time and again throughout the ages. And given the history of banditry attributed to Brennan's inhabitants, it would likely prove effective there too.

Such simplicity. Bandits craved money and loot, and both were things the armored king could promise in exchange for Brennan's support. Now the question was how much their asking price would be. The only way to find out was to get there and make the offer.

#

Riorik, along with the help of Asbin's father, had managed to convince the others that they needed to give chase to the retreating horde before their enemies could find shelter or rendezvous with more soldiers. Several hours had already passed since the horde fled Mechii, but the gnomes were determined to secure their homes before they'd even consider

venturing forth. Likewise, several of the dwarves demanded that word be

sent to Rhorm to call for reinforcements. Asbin's father resisted the

demands of his fellow dwarves at first but eventually acquiesced on the

condition that they wouldn't wait for the reinforcements to arrive before

chasing down the.

Once that had finally been agreed upon, the next obstacle reared its head.

The defense of Mechii had taken a toll on the survivors who were too

battle-weary and hungry to march on such short notice. Many of the new

alliance called for the group to take advantage of their proximity of the

gnome town by eating a meal there and taking a quick rest. It was one

excuse after another it seemed. They were without a unified command

structure, as the alliance was only held together by shared agreement, so

there was little anyone could do but negotiate with each other to achieve

the best outcome possible.

In the end, Riorik and the others were able to negotiate an agreement. The allies decided that since night had already fallen and trying to track the horde in the dark would be difficult for some, they would spend the remainder of the night at Mechii, where everyone could do as they pleased. It was up to the individuals to eat, sleep, mend their wounds, sharpen their blades, or whatever else they wanted to spend that time doing, but at first light, the group would proceed—no matter what. Riorik and his friends could do little but wait. Riorik initially thought that scouting ahead might be their best option, but the hunger pains that grew in his stomach quickly made him think better of it. Their visit to Rishdel had been all too brief, giving the elves little time to restock their supplies or even enjoy a good homecooked meal, something Riorik had looked forward to sharing with his mother at the time. Now, the prospect of sitting down to share a real meal after the day's efforts appealed not just to Riorik but to his friends too.

Gary Richardson

Ammudien led Riorik, Nordahs, and Rory into Mechii's shop district, which had stayed open late to serve the brave fighters who'd defended the city. There were many options, some familiar, some not, for the friends to pick from. Various breads, dried fruits, and dried meats were shoved into their pouches. The merchants offered the group generous discounts for the goods, and they gladly and eagerly paid with the remaining coin taken from the fallen bandits at the camp outside Tyleco. With the last of their coin, the pack of friends purchased a feast of fresh food from the vendors. They sat around in a circle, passing the various bowls, plates, and mugs back and forth as they all shared the same food. The sweet and savory smells that wafted from each dish seemed only to fuel their hunger more. Each ate at a feverous pace, slurping, gulping, and smacking on every drop and morsel that touched their lips, careful not to spill a drop or crumb. To an onlooker, it might appear as if nobody in the group had eaten for days, which was not too far from the truth. Riorik couldn't recall when they'd last had a decent meal.

Eventually, the feasting slowed and conversation resumed. The food was gone and with it, their hunger. Now, the group took turns complaining about how miserable they felt and how they couldn't fight even if they had to. It didn't take long for that misery to turn into tiredness. One by one, each of the four adventures lay down with their full bellies and drifted off for a well-deserved rest.

Before long, the morning arrived. Their rest was brief but effective as the group awoke to the bells clanging in the Mage Academy's tallest ivory tower, signaling the start of a new day. The agreement had been made that now was the time to start their pursuit of Riorik's father and his army, but first, Riorik had to wake those who did not stir at the bell's sounding. It took several minutes to wake those who'd drunk too much in their celebrations or who were simply not eager to wake up at such an early hour. Eventually, the masses were raised from their slumber and once more gathered at the entrance to the gnome city. Word had no doubt reached Rhorm by now to send reinforcements so more dwarves should be close behind.

Each group nominated a member to represent them at the vanguard. Naturally, Riorik represented his party. Villkir stood for the barbarians. Much to Riorik's surprise, the gnomes voted Ammudien to be their steward since he had the most experience in this particular arena. But unsurprising was the appointment of Asbin's father, Yafic[2] Firehammer, to lead the dwarves.

Each group would act as a separate force, answering only to that group's appointed leader. Any coordinated effort would be up to the four leaders to decide upon and relay to their troops. Everyone recognized that some semblance of order was needed to fight such a foe, but given their time constraints, this was the best command structure everyone could agree on.

---

[2] Pronounced "Yeah-fick"

Fed, rested, prepared, and organized, the group set out from Mechii anxious to pick up the horde's trail and bring this failed invasion to an end.

#

It was mid-day by the time the horde reached the gates of Brennan. Though most towns left their gates open during the day, the gates of Brennan always remained closed—partly so the guards could extort people wanting entry to the city, and partly to keep out any bandits who failed to pay their dues to the bandit king in exchange for using Brennan as a place of hiding or a base of operations.

The bandit king, Draynard, demanded a tax to be paid by all bandits who operated outside of his operation. Even those who worked for Draynard were required to turn over the majority of their loot to him, keeping only a small percentage for themselves. Draynard had lost many bandits to Malick's band of thieves, given that Malick shared the loot more evenly with his brothers, but Malick lacked the ability to offer respite inside a secure city. That was advantage enough to allow Draynard to demand more from those looking to him for protection and work. He was the only

bandit leader who could call an entire city his own.

And now, there was a massive force at his city's gate, looking to gain

entrance.

"We have an offer to put before your city's leadership," one of the humans

among the horde called out to the watchmen along the top of the city's

wall.

The elven king decided it would be best to have another human make the

offer, or at least open negotiations, thinking that an offer from one human

to another would return less resistance than if the offer came from

another of the many races that made up the horde's body.

"And what offer is that?" one of the guards called back from his spot atop

the wall.

"We wish to make the offer directly to your leaders—and your leaders

only," the human replied from his position among the horde. "Just allow

us entry into the city so that we may make our offer."

"Ah, yes, well, that would be a problem then," the guard replied.

"How so?" the confused human shouted back.

"Well, you see, our beloved King Draynard is not currently in the city, so there would be little value in you coming in," the guard sarcastically answered.

"And where is your King Draynard then? Perhaps we should journey to his location to make our offer there instead," the horde's representative said, pressing the guard for more information.

"There's no need for that. King Draynard is here," the guard answered.

"How's that? Are you intentionally being rude? You just said that he was gone!" the irritated human shouted back.

"Oh, nay. I said he was not in the city. If you wish to speak to King Draynard, you only need turn around," the guard replied with a big grin flashing across his lips.

Those among the horde had all heard the guard's response but were unsure what to make of it. They'd traveled here from Mechii expecting to be followed, so those near the rear routinely checked for pursuers, but not a soul had been seen. Many assumed the guard's statement was some trick or a ploy to distract them while the guards rained down arrows. Others assumed it was some kind of metaphor that suggested King Draynard was more of a concept and not a real person.

But the horde's elven leader was unconcerned about a rear assault and knew that King Draynard was more than some existential metaphor. The armored elf with his shiny green breastplate glinting in the day's growing light spun on his heels and made his way to the rear of the horde. His soldiers quickly cleared a path for him, careful not to get in his way. It didn't take him long to traverse the now-diminished horde, and once at the rear, the looked upon the face of King Draynard, the human bandit who controlled Brennan, and the bandit king's guard.

"I was wondering how long it would take you to arrive," Draynard said to the horde's leader. "We were growing tired of following you at such a slow pace throughout the night."

"Oh, I beg to differ. We were not followed," the Macadrian king said in disbelief.

"I assure you that you were," Draynard said with seriousness. "We watched as you and your troops were routed at Mechii and again as you turned tail to run away from a few horses. You cannot bring an army of this size into this land without me and my spies catching wind of it."

"So, your spies informed you of our less than stellar battle results. It still does little to prove we were followed," the elf proclaimed, desperate to regain a position of authority that now rested with Draynard.

"My good sir, we are thieves. We make it our business not to be seen. Do not fret or be angry with your rear guard. We're good at our trade, and if we meant you harm, we could've easily picked off several of your troops along the way. Now, your herald spoke of an offer. May we put the past behind us and speak of our futures instead?"

There was a glint in Draynard's eye as he thought about the potential loot he could extort from his newest target.

Gary Richardson

#

Riorik and Nordahs, being the only trained Rangers in the group, decided

to scout ahead of the others to find the horde's trail and keep it fresh. The

trail had led north for a good way, leading away from the failed assault on

Mechii. There were a few tracks that split off from the main group, but it

wasn't clear if these were deserters, scouts, hunters, or messengers. There

could be any number of reasons for these departures.

Regardless, Riorik and Nordahs were easily able to follow the tracks and

trampled trail of vegetation left behind by the still massive force. The two

Rangers were certain that the horde was headed back to Kern, and the

tracks seemed to prove them right—until they did not.

Riorik and Nordahs reached the spot where the invaders encountered

Lord Veyron and his forces. Nordahs was the first to recognize the new

tracks, while Riorik was focused on the strange skid mark in the middle,

the mark left from his father's collision with the lance-wielding rider. The track left by the brief fight was unusual, and Riorik struggled to make

sense of it, leaving Nordahs free to follow the horse tracks.

"They ran into a pack of horses with riders here," Nordahs said as he

studied the hoof prints left in the soft soil. "I don't think they were friendly

towards one another. Your father's troops look to have turned west, and

the horses fled north at high speed."

"Was it some kind of stand-off?" Riorik asked, his curiosity piqued at

Nordahs' assessment.

"No, there was a fight," Nordahs replied as he found one of the horde's

fallen troops.

The body had been half-eaten by scavengers and dragged away from

where the conflict actually happened, but Nordahs could still make out the

wounds inflicted during the fight, obvious signs that there'd been some

kind of struggle at this location recently. Plus, the keen-eyed elven Ranger

had spotted the shattered remains of a knight's lance. He picked up a few of the wooden shards and studied them, looking for clues, but he found none that made sense.

"Take a look at this," Riorik called to his friend, pointing out the odd skid mark in the dirt. "What do you make of this?"

"It looks like somebody slid across the ground to me," Nordahs said in a matter-of-fact tone, assessing the obvious nature of the impression left behind by their prey.

"Yeah, it certainly looks that way, but look at how deep the impression is. It would take a tremendous amount of force or weight to cause a mark like that in this ground. The group fled Mechii with no heavy equipment, and we haven't seen any other trails like this along the way. This one track is unique to this spot. It doesn't make sense to me."

"They did encounter some mounted riders. Maybe a horse left this mark?" Nordahs said questioningly as he bent down to take a closer look at the mark.

"This is not a horse," Riorik instantly rebutted his friend's suggestion. "If a horse had slid here, there would be marks for all four hooves and with wider separation than what we see here. This is definitely the mark of something on two legs, not four. And do you see the lack of detail in the track? There are no signs of individual toes, but there's a rounded tip here. These looks like the marks of armor-covered feet, and based on the size, I would assume either an elf or a human made these marks."

"Yeah, maybe, but that wouldn't make sense. How and why would an elf or a human make marks like that in the dirt?" Nordahs asked, accepting Riorik's accurate assessment of the track but still not understanding it.

"I can't say," Riorik started, "but all I know is that whatever caused this track would've required a lot of force. More force than either of us could generate or tolerate."

"So, you think whoever made this mark was killed by it?" Nordahs asked his friend.

"Surprisingly, no," Riorik answered. "The marks come to a solid end and look to dig in a bit more here, like the skidding motion stopped. I think the force that caused the skid was now reflected back in the direction it came from. And, look here! You can see armored boot marks that match the size and shape of these depressions leading away from here. They move to the west, the same direction as the rest of the army. It looks like whoever made these marks not only survived but walked away."

"Do you think it was your father?"

"It's the only answer that makes sense. The breastplate gives him such good protection and increases his strength. If anybody's going to take a hit like that and walk away, it would have to be him."

"Well, that might explain why the horses ran away so quickly," Nordahs added.

"The trail heads to the west, but they're still a few hours ahead of us," Riorik stated as he finally moved on from the strange mark and continued studying the area.

"If we don't hurry, they could destroy another town," Nordahs added worryingly.

"Agreed. We should go back and tell the others and encourage them to pick up the pace," Riorik suggested.

"Why don't you go back and spread the message while I continue to scout ahead to make sure that they didn't change direction again. The last thing we need is for them to try and circle back to a largely undefended Mechii or Rhorm now," Nordahs countered.

"And that right there is why we work so well as a team, Nord," Riorik said with a grin, grateful for his friend's input. "You always seem to find the flaws in my plans before I do, and thankfully, before we put it into action. I like your plan better than my own. Be careful. I'll catch up to you as soon as I can."

The two friends clasped hands firmly, coupled with a few nods and words of reassurance. It was the first time since the pair had set out from Rishdel at the start their quest that they'd split up and gone in different directions.

Riorik was apprehensive about sending his best friend off after the horde alone, but his own position of leadership among the newly formed alliance would be critical for speeding up their rate of movement. Riorik's plan might've been safer for Nordahs, but Riorik also knew that Nordahs' plan was safest for everyone else.

With their concerns and fears buried deep down, afraid to speak about them out of fear they may come true, the two elves parted ways. Riorik headed back towards their allies and friends who followed a short distance behind, while Nordahs turned west to continue following the invaders.

Chapter 4

As Lord Veyron and his men rode along the road back to Tyleco, they approached Kern once more. They were met by a familiar face as they approached the city. It was the scrawny man who was among the group of citizens that had confronted them about the desecration of Lord Shiron's body. This time, however, the pale, skinny man was alone. His bigger, bald friend was nowhere to be seen, and the lone man appeared to move with a limp in his step that they hadn't noticed during their last encounter with him.

"You must turn back!" the man urged Lord Veyron as he approached the mounted lord of Tyleco.

"What is the meaning of this?" Lord Veyron questioned the odd individual.

The frail-looking man hobbled nearer to Lord Veyron's position before the lord's guards cut him off, using their crossed lances to create a barricade. The man huffed and puffed under the strain of moving about with his weakened limbs as he held onto the lances.

"Kern is not safe to you or anyone who supports you," the man gasped between breaths.

"Explain," Lord Veyron demanded, uninterested in the man's exhaustion or his wounds.

"The dark one did not take all of his troops with him when they moved south. Some remained in Kern to ensure our obedience. We were seen speaking with you before they interrogated us, and they wanted to know what was said. My friend, Balmor[3], the bald guy, refused to talk, so they tied him to a post and used a horse to rip out his tongue. They left him there to bleed to death! The rest of us were beaten until they got what they wanted. My life is in grave danger even talking to you now."

"How many of his troops remain in Kern? Could my men free your people from their oppression?" Lord Veyron asked, always looking for opportunities to gain new supporters to back him in his claim to the throne.

"Doubtful. The troops that remain are fewer than those that marched on, but there's still significant in number. Besides, they await his return soon." Lord Veyron laughed at the mention of the army's expected return.

"There will be no swift return. That disheveled mob of an army was redirected by my men just hours ago. They now head west, away from Kern. If the rabble remaining in Kern are anything like the pathetic so-

---

[3] Pronounced "Bahl-mor"

called soldiers we saw, then we should have little work rousting them from your homes."

Lord Veyron was careful not to mention the armor's existence or even the armored elf's ability to withstand a direct charge from his knight. He knew that the only reason the masked leader survived was due to the power of the armor that protected him. None of the other soldiers had such power, so he felt there was little to fear from anyone else.

Of course, Lord Veyron's words did pass without notice from his own troops. There were several silent glances shared between them. Only Lord Veyron among them understood the full weight of the events that they'd all witnessed. The rest of his cavalry were left in a state of shock and awe at what they'd seen. Great fear was struck in the hearts of many Tyleco soldiers, who now questioned how such an army could be defeated—but none dared say that to Lord Veyron.

"As encouraging as that is," the thin man began, "I still do not think it's safe for you to attempt to liberate Kern. There are still several skilled archers and other infantry who've taken up residence in the city's keep.

Not to mention the people of Kern who support them. Please, I beseech

you, return to Tyleco and forget Kern for the time being."

The man's words were concerning to Lord Veyron. His ambition to claim

the throne urged him to march on Kern despite the warnings, but deep

down, he knew that now was not the time. With the self-proclaimed king's

larger force roaming the lands and multiple pieces of the Ascension Armor

known to be involved, Lord Veyron knew that his priority and obligation

was to take on the army's main force, not those stationed at Kern.

"Well," Lord Veyron began his reply, "rest assured that we will not ride to

Kern today. We're returning to Tyleco to muster my remaining forces so

that we may take the fight to your oppressor's main force. Once we have

vanquished that lot, we will return and free you from the shackles of

slavery and brutality that you have no doubt suffered under their reign."

"Oh, thank you, my lord," the man professed his gratitude, having heard

that Lord Veyron planned on returning to Tyleco.

The two guards uncrossed their lances, sending the man stumbling backward, as they returned to their position in the formation. Lord Veyron gave a nod to the others to signal it was time for them to move on. The cavalry units thundered past the scrawny resident of Kern on their way back to Tyleco.

What Lord Veyron and his men didn't know was that the skinny man was the one who'd caved under the punishment and interrogation of those in Kern loyal to the northern king. His purpose for approaching Lord Veyron was very different than the mounted ruler of Tyleco had assumed or believed. In fact, the deathly thin man from Kern had intentionally gone out to speak with Lord Veyron to gain information to report back to his new oppressors. There was concern growing in Kern by the northern soldiers left behind, given their leader's absolute confidence of a quick victory, but nobody had returned to Kern or even sent word via messenger or bird.

With the knowledge that the dark army had been sent fleeing from Lord Veyron's forces to the west, the resident-turned-informant ran back to the city gates once he was certain Lord Veyron and his men had ridden far enough away. Once inside the gates, the man. who many would consider a traitor to Kern, slunk through the city's streets as he made his way to the keep, where most of the troops had taken up residence.

The skinny informant wasted no time in informing the leaders who'd been left to oversee Kern of the current situation. It wasn't welcomed news, but the troops were grateful to the spineless resident regardless. The lieutenant who'd been left in charge rewarded the man with a small stack of coins and encouraged the skinny man to use his new windfall to buy himself some food. The scrawny man only nodded in agreement before backing out of the room, greedily clutching his reward as though someone were about to kill him and take it back.

\#

Riorik, still concerned about his friend's safety, made haste in his return to the group headed out from Mechii in pursuit of the fleeing horde. The young elven Ranger explained the situation to the others, explaining how they'd found signs of an encounter with horses, likely those of Lord Veyron's men, based on their own previous encounter with the human leader, and how the tracks turned west. Riorik also made certain to point out that Nordahs had continued onward to locate and possibly monitor the horde alone, while Riorik returned to them.

"We must hurry to catch Nordahs before he runs into them on his own. He's by himself out there, and I do not wish to find my friend dead because I moved too slowly," he said as he tried to urge the others to pick up their pace.

There was some hesitation and consternation from the others regarding the news and Riorik's desire to move faster.

"Many of these people are not trained soldiers with your level of conditioning," Ammudien Flickerspell reminded Riorik. "Just look at the gnomes here. Most of them spend their time studying, researching, and sitting down. Long marches and heavy fighting is new to them, not to mention the fact that for every step you take, it takes them at least twice as many to keep up. If you move at a faster pace, it will be almost impossible for me and my people to keep up, especially over a long distance."

Yafic was the next to speak up. "I have to agree with my fellow short guy here," the old dwarf started. "We dwarves are known for our stamina but not for our speed. We may not tire out as fast as our pointy-eared friends here, but there's no way we'd be able to keep up with you and your long-legged friends. There's a limit to how fast this pack can move, and it must be at our pace, not yours."

The reality of their words hit Riorik like a giant weight on his chest. The exasperation and desperation were obvious in the fine features of his face. The normally smooth, almost porcelain-like skin was wrinkled around his brow, and his thin lips turned down in a frown. He needed another plan, but nothing was coming to him at this moment. Riorik's couldn't think beyond his fear of Nordahs facing off against their enemy and the invading army on his own.

"I understand your concerns," Yafic continued, seeing the elf's struggles outlined so plainly across his face, "so why don't we do this? You take the barbarians and your human friend and hurry along after your buddy. That way, he won't be alone should he run into those fiends before we have a chance to catch up and finish them off. Ammudien and I will follow behind as best as we can. If we make our people try to keep up with you now, when it comes time to fight, we'll all be too pooped to help. This way, even if we show up after the fighting starts, we'll at least still be prepared to fight instead of being there from the beginning but being a hindrance instead of a help."

Overwhelmed by his emotions, Riorik's thoughts were not as focused as usual, which prompted him to ask a question that he should've known the answer to already.

"Sure, but if we run ahead, how will you all be able to find us? I mean, if we're that much faster than you, won't you have a hard time knowing where we are?"

Ammudien could only chuckle at Riorik's temporary ignorance.

"Fool, have you forgotten how we found the armor to begin with? If we need a direction to go, we have an army of mages to detect not only your armor but also the pieces of the armor your father carries. You can run as far ahead as you need to, and I assure you, we'll be able to follow. Now, go to Nordahs. We've already lost Wuffred—let's not lose another."

Riorik was embarrassed that he hadn't thought of the gnome's ability to track the magic that helped to make the Ascension Armor. He was so consumed with thoughts of his friend and his father that the obvious things were somehow shrouded from him. He apologized to his gnome friend, who willingly accepted the elf's words but again encouraged him to leave.

Having apologized several times, Riorik led the barbarians and Rory off towards the direction he expected Nordahs to be headed. His plan was to intersect Nordahs along the horde's trail to the west, but his plan assumed that the other forces hadn't deviated from that path. Either way, Riorik would either find his friend or pick up his trail.

He led his portion of the defenders off in a northwestern direction, the path he expected to find his friend on, and maybe his father.

#

The old elf from the post office in Rishdel strode up to Elder Bostic's seat at the head table in the Guildhall's mess with nary a care. For the Rangers, it was considered a great taboo to interrupt the elders while they ate, but the old elf, who was not a Ranger, didn't think twice about his actions. The elderly postmaster walked with purpose and determination as he approached the head table, only stopping once he stood directly opposite of Elder Bostic.

The white-haired elder finished his current bite before stopping to look at the postmaster. He started to speak, but the old post keeper spoke first.

"This is for you. It's important," he said as he held out his hand containing a small message scroll.

The elder took the small scroll and unrolled it before reading its contents.

'A large force has been seen moving west, south of Tyleco. Brennan is all that stands between them and Rishdel. Ready your defenses. Reports indicate that Dresden was annihilated. Brennan may not be able to resist long.'

The scroll had been sealed with the stamp of Rishdel, marking it as coming from one of the guild's reconnaissance scouts that were dispatched by the elders after Riorik and Nordahs left.

The elders hadn't wanted to inspire fear in others by acting rashly or publicly, so instead they'd discreetly sent various senior Rangers out beyond the forest's border to survey the situation and report back.

Most of the reports confirmed what the young elves had said about a large force marching towards Kern. Another report mentioned the fall of Kern. And another highlighted the broken window in Lord Veyron's grand hall. However, none of them mentioned the horde or its approach towards Rishdel before now.

Before Elder Bostic could fully process the scroll's meaning, much less share the news with the other elders eating with him, another elf walked through the door. This young female elf wore similar clothes to the postmaster's. She was his assistant and helped him send and receive messages from the small post office.

The young elf was also in charge of taking care of the birds, feeding them, tending to them, nursing any injuries, and just looking after them, in general, to ensure that Rishdel always had healthy, well-kept birds to send messages with. The elves were keen on making sure their messenger birds looked regal. They didn't want the other races to mock them for using birds of questionable appearance or condition.

The young female elf hurried across the room but remained silent. There were strict rules and protocols regarding the presence of non-Rangers in the Guildhall that she was keenly aware of. For her to yell out would be a sign of disrespect to the Rangers and the elders. It was even considered disrespectful for Rangers of lower ranks to speak at any volume higher than they'd use in speaking to their neighbors. The only ones allowed to speak in loud tones were the higher-ranking Rangers and the elders, with the elders' voices overruling everyone else.

"Another message arrived right after you left," she whispered to the old postmaster as she handed him the latest scroll.

"And couldn't this have waited until my return?" he asked her in a similar hushed tone, annoyed by her disruption and presence.

"It seemed related to the message that brought you here, so I figured you'd want it immediately," the young female elf answered meekly, though she began to second-guess her decision.

The postmaster took the scroll and examined it. His eyes widened at the scroll's content before turning back to Elder Bostic.

"Elder Bostic, you will want to see this one too," he said as he handed the elven elder the new message.

The elder looked at the scroll with great concern. The seal on this one was that of Rhorm, not Rishdel. The dwarven seal caught the elder's attention and piqued his curiosity. Elder Bostic unrolled this scroll to see what it had to add to the situation.

'A force of invaders was repelled from Rhorm and Mechii. A united army from our towns, with the help of Riorik and Nordahs, pursue the army, but the army is in possession of items of great power. Please dispatch the Rangers to aid them in defending this land from those who would see us all dead or enslaved. Time is of the essence. We repelled their assault once, but I fear they will return in greater numbers unless we act together to counter the force they bring to bear against us.*

Riorik and Nordahs saved me when I needed help, but now I am in no condition to help them directly, so I am trying to aid them the only other way I can. Please help them as they helped me.

-Asbin Firehammer'

Asbin had received word about the recent events, and even in her very pregnant state, she was determined to do all she could for her friends. When the call was sent back to Rhorm to round up the remaining fighters to pursue the horde, Asbin was eager to join but knew her place was at Rhorm.

Instead, she made sure to glean as much information from those who'd been involved. She knew knowledge was just as powerful as her weapon was, and she vowed to make an equal impact in the battle with what she'd learned instead.

The dwarven healer still held her fair share of resentment for the Rangers after what she heard they'd done to Wuffred and Riorik during their time at the guild, but she knew that if the Rangers joined the fight, there would be better odds of success. She'd had to swallow her pride and her anger to pen such a message for the elven elders. In her condition, her emotions ran high and her skin thin, so it was not an easy task, but Asbin managed to complete the note without a single snide comment or any hint of complaint about their treatment of those she cared about.

Now, it was up to Elder Bostic to decide what to do with this information. Would he dispatch the Rangers to help fight the Horde? Would he keep the Rangers in Rishdel and instead focus on defending the village? Would the elves even believe Asbin's message? There was nothing for the dwarf to do, no way to find out except to wait.

Chapter 5

"Why don't we take this discussion somewhere more comfortable," the

armored king suggested to Draynard.

The two leaders stood face to face outside the city walls of Brennan, but

the king from Narsdin was eager to find shelter behind Draynard's walls

and men. Their recent defeats at Rhorm and Mechii had made him nervous, to say the least, and he didn't want to leave himself or his troops exposed any longer than necessary.

But Draynard was no fool.

"If you and I would like to speak somewhere more private, then the two of us may adjourn to more comfortable settings, but your troops will remain here until we have reached an accord," the bandit king countered.

Draynard's words incensed the invader. He was unaccustomed to being told no by anyone. The last individual to tell him no was King Pan, the kobold leader who'd refused to offer troops to aid in his invasion. In retribution, the northern king had sabotaged the ship that Pan used to sail home to the island of Do'ricka.

But this was different. This time, the northern king was not safe behind his own walls but instead exposed and vulnerable outside of Draynard's. The armored elf was forced to hold his tongue—and his sword.

There was still much to learn about Draynard's true military prowess and might. The elven leader with dreams of conquest didn't know how many other bandits remained hidden or what types of defenses might lie in wait within the city. He had already underestimated the capabilities of the dwarves and gnomes. Those underestimations are what had led him here to Brennan.

To make a similar mistake by attacking a third enemy he knew too little about would almost certainly be a death sentence, especially now they'd lost the element of surprise. Even with the power bestowed on him by the armor, there was no other real option but to concede to Draynard's demands.

But maybe not fully, not just yet.

"Would you at least be open to allowing me to station a lookout atop your wall? You know that we're pursued by those who also persecute your people, so a lookout would help to reassure me that my troops won't be taken by surprise while we're in negotiations."

Draynard took a moment to contemplate the armored one's request. He looked over the king's remaining troops and evaluated the risks of each member. The trolls and orcs were big and strong. Even one of them inside the city could spell disaster for Draynard's men, but they had poor eyesight compared to others in the invading force, so it would be unlikely, or at least unwise, for the king to position one of them in the city if the intent was truly to act as a lookout.

Next, Draynard spied several humans among the troops. These he felt might blend in too easily with the city's inhabitants and be capable of carrying out acts of subterfuge.

Then, he spied the dark elves. King Draynard, having had dealings with other dark elves as part of his bandit empire, knew the dark elves to have excellent eyesight but to also be extremely ruthless and often deceitful.

And finally, he looked upon the gnolls. Draynard knew they could be vicious fighters, like the dark elves, especially when backed into a corner. The gnolls also had great vision that made them excellent choices as lookouts.

None of them were ideal candidates to be left alone in his city, but Draynard recognized the strengths and weaknesses of each. In the end, he resolved to wait and see who the other leader suggested as his lookout, which might reveal any dubious intentions his guest may have.

"I will allow one lookout to enter with us but not more than one, and I have to approve of your selection," Draynard finally answered.

The bandit king's words stung the impatient king of Macadre, but he knew there was a great risk to himself and his troops if he were to defy Draynard, or even worse, attack him, as his emotions tempted him to do. The armored king looked among his ranks and took stock of who remained. His mind raced with ideas for how to use each one. Deep down, he wanted an orc or a troll in the city to be nearer his location in case Draynard attempted some kind of deceit of his own. The orc would be a formidable foe who could likely break down the gate and allow the other troops to come to the king's rescue, but as a lookout, he knew the orc to be weak. With the threat of pursuers, a poor lookout could spell disaster for his troops, and then who would come to his aid if the negotiations with the bandit king broke down? No, the orcs were out, as were the trolls for the same reason.

However, when it came to the humans among his ranks, the armored king felt it best to leave them outside the city for a completely different reason than Draynard's. The bandit king was afraid the humans in the northern forces could blend in with the humans who made up the majority of the residents in Brennan and carry out acts of terrorism or sabotage. But the armored elf was actually afraid that his human troops may abandon his cause and seek refuge among their fellow humans, leaving the other troops vulnerable outside the city's walls. This left only the dark elves and gnolls for the Macadrian king to pick from, which, for a lookout, made the most sense anyway.

This was a tough decision for the would-be conqueror. The two groups, dark elves, and gnolls, had similar strengths and weaknesses that made them equal in his eyes. Neither group would be well liked or welcomed among the humans, even bandits. But both groups offered superior eyesight that would be ideal for a lookout and both were nimble, agile fighters who could hold their own against the bandits, at least for a short while. That would be useful in case the two leaders failed to come to an agreement that would offer the armored king a longer-term level of protection or perhaps an alliance of the two groups.

In the end, Narsdin's king settled on a dark elf to act as his lookout. He figured, and quite correctly, that if given the choice between accepting a dark elf or a gnoll, the human bandits would be more receptive to an elf since they shared a more common set of features and attributes compared to the dog-like features of the gnolls.

Now, all that was left to do was to pick which dark elf would be given the task. Eager not to waste any more time, time their pursuers could use to move closer without detection, the armored elf picked the first dark elf his eyes landed on among the horde's masses.

"That one," he said to Draynard as he pointed out the unsuspecting elf, an act that made the dark elf extremely nervous since he had no idea why he was being singled out by his master.

He tried to look brave and strong as he fearfully left his position of safety and anonymity among the horde and approached his beckoning king.

"Y-y-yes, my liege?" the dark elf said hesitantly as he approached.

"Your orders are simple," the armored king said as he began his reply. "King Draynard and I have business to discuss in the city. While we talk, you're to take up a position along the top of Brennan's outer wall among King Draynard's men and perform lookout duty. If you see any threats to my army, you're to alert them immediately and then come find me."

"But," the bandit king quickly said, interrupting this guest, "while you're there, do not act in any way that my men may find threatening or dubious. You are a guest in Brennan and expected to act accordingly, unless you want my men to separate your head from your shoulders."

Again, Draynard's words stung the ambitious king's ears. The bandit king openly threatened his troops, but there was nothing he could say or do about it at the moment. The armored elf was once more forced to let what he perceived as an indignity towards him pass by without response or reprimand.

Feelings of anger and heightened emotions aside, the deal was eventually struck, but not before the armored king tried one more thing.

"And what of my own protection? Should I not have at least one guard accompany me?" the northern king asked at the last moment, eager to get his troops behind the city's gate.

"There's no need for that," Draynard responded. "I will ensure your safety while you remain in my company."

The question had also annoyed the bandit king. It was obvious what his guest was trying to do, despite Draynard's earlier assertions. The bandit king didn't appreciate someone trying to manipulate him, and he easily recognized the armored elf's attempt to do just that.

"I thought we were here to talk business, king to king. If you think you can play me for a fool in hopes of stealing my city out of from under my control, then you're wrong. Dead wrong," he said to his guest, emphasizing the word 'dead'.

"Now," Draynard continued, "if you wish to continue our negotiations, then you and your single lookout can follow me into my city. But if your plan is to continue trying to undermine my authority in my own city, then I can leave you and your troops here to rot, and if I'm so inclined, my troops will see to it that rot is exactly what happens to your corpses, even before those who follow you make it here."

Draynard's words and tone made it abundantly clear to the invader that the bandit king was not amused by his efforts and that their already strained relationship was teetering on the edge of disaster. While the armored king was cut off from the troops remaining in Kern and without his siege weapons, he was forced to take Draynard's threats more seriously than they would've been otherwise. There was no recourse for the northern king but to apologize and relent once and for all to Draynard's demands before entering the city gates and disappearing behind them, leaving his troops exposed and vulnerable outside.

#

The guards near the gates of Tyleco instantly recognized their lord's banners flying among the cavalry as Lord Veyron and his knights rapidly approached. The guards hurried to open the gates, knowing Lord Veyron didn't like to wait to enter his city. The large wooden doors were swung open as men pushed from the outside while those inside pulled. They wanted to ensure that not only were the gates opened but that they were opened wide enough to allow the whole cavalry easy passage.

The horses and their riders stormed through the gate and down the cobblestone streets that weaved throughout the city as they made their way back towards the keep.

"Assemble at the keep! All troops of Tyleco muster now!" the knights commanded as they sped through the gates, past the guardhouse, and along the city streets.

The shouted orders sparked a flurry of activity. Guards outside the gates ran inside while the multitude of guards that patrolled the city ran towards the large stone keep near the rear of the city. Guard after guard poured out of the guardhouse and followed the others.

The only men who didn't turn and hustle towards the keep were those tasked with keeping watch. It was standing orders from Lord Veyron himself that even during a muster call to all troops, the wall remain manned and the city's perimeter monitored. This, of course, could be overturned at any time, but only by Lord Veyron, who hadn't issued such a decree as he rode through the gate.

Lord Veyron and his mounted knights waited outside the keep's entrance while the remaining troops throughout the city continued to gather nearby. Lord Veyron observed the rows of assembling troops from under his helmet's visor with a stern and serious face. He was still angry about Ammudien and Rory's escape with the legendary shield, but now he was more concerned about the display of power from the elf wearing Trylon's breastplate and the horde the elf traveled with.

Eventually, the troops had largely gathered around their leader. Many noticed his armor was not the usual shiny steel but showed signs of scorching, thanks to Ammudien and Kirin's magic. None dared to ask or point out the disheveled look of Lord Veyron's armor, but they couldn't hide the whispers that spread among their ranks.

"Silence!" Lord Veyron demanded, determined to stop the comments and theories spreading about his armor's shabby look. Even the normally very organized and professional knights now looked rattled.

The noise rising from within the group came to an immediate end.

"A great and dangerous evil has found its way into our lands," Lord Veyron began once he was satisfied he had his men's attention. "It's our duty to defend our city and our people from such threats. My knights and I successfully defended an approach by this group towards our great city, but our enemy fled west. Now, it's our duty to rally together and head off this threat before they circle back and try to take Tyleco by force. Let us take the fight to our enemy before they bring the fight to our home!"

Lord Veyron was careful not to mention that their enemy's leader had been able to withstand a direct blow from one of his knight's lances. He was also careful to leave out any mention of the Ascension Armor and their enemy's possession of at least one piece. The human leader was interested in inspiring his troops to his cause, not scaring them into abandoning their posts.

What the usually inspiring leader said and left unsaid successfully roused the enthusiasm of his troops. The assortment of infantry, archers, and scouts erupted loudly in support of Lord Veyron and voiced their outrage against the threat. Several of the troops hoisted their weapons into the air, creating a sea of swords, axes, hammers, maces, polearms, and bows.

Having successfully rallied his troops, Lord Veyron began to lead them from the city once more.

"Onward to victory! Onward to honor!" Lord Veyron shouted as his full army marched beyond the city's gate before stopping to issue one final order.

"You lot up there," he shouted to the few remaining lookouts still stationed along the city's grand wall. "Be sure to keep your eyes to the north and watch for any reinforcements approaching from that direction. I have no desire to be stabbed in the back on the field of battle while defending your lives."

The soldiers on the wall saluted their leader and shouted in unison to acknowledge his orders before promptly returning to their duties.

"In the name of Tyleco and our families, we march!" Lord Veyron shouted at his troops, nudging his horse to a slight trot forward.

As the army moved past the gates and outside the city, they did not move east towards Kern as they had before. No, this time, Lord Veyron circled his troops to the west. He was well aware of the river that separated the lands between Tyleco and Brennan, but the bandit town was almost a direct march south from Tyleco across the plains that divided the two towns. It was a much more direct and faster march than if he led his troops along the roads west to Kern and then south towards Mechii and the only traversable bridge over the river outside of the forest surrounding Rishdel.

Lord Veyron was eager to confront the new enemy and hopefully acquire the breastplate of lore for himself. If the army marched towards Brennan, there was a real risk that it could fall into the hands of another rival to Lord Veyron's claim—Draynard. Lord Veyron wasn't going to let that happen, so he made sure to choose the most direct path to intersect with the foreign army and the object of his latest desire.

The leader from Tyleco was aware his men would have to cross the the fast flowing river that separated his lands from those of Brennan, but it was a risk he was willing to take to move closer to his goal of being crowned king once and for all.

#

The gates of Kern opened wide for the first time since Lord Shiron's act of cowardice, followed by his death at the hands of the invaders. But unlike the last time the gates were opened like this, troops were marching out of the city instead of within.

The news of Lord Veyron's encounter with their master's troops and the troop's redirection to the west was enough to spur those who remained in Kern to act. As a group, the leaders of Kern all agreed that if their master had been forced to turn away from the city, then it was their duty to deploy reinforcements to aid him in battle.

After hearing their informant's description of Lord Veyron's knights—in particular, the scant number of knights he rode with compared to their master's forces—there was concern and fear among them that the battles at Mechii and Rhorm had gone terribly awry. They concluded that if there ever was a time that their powerful leader would need their help, it was now. The walking corpse of a man who had informed them didn't know how successful the other raids had been, but his repeated assurances that Lord Veyron claimed to have forced the great army away led the leaders of Kern to draw those conclusions for themselves.

The reinforcements were devoid of wargs, warg-riders, orcs, and trolls, and seemed much smaller compared to the forces that marched out of Kern just recently. In truth, their numbers were smaller than the main army's by about half, and because they lacked the over-sized orcs and trolls, the group looked much smaller than it actually was.

This group consisted of fighters trained in the art of warfare more so than the main army, whose purpose was to shock and awe with an overwhelming show of force. These soldiers were the real fighting force of the army hailing from Narsdin, and they knew it.

At the front marched several rows of troops carrying pikes and polearms that could be used to defend themselves from mounted knights that might otherwise try to charge through and break up their ranks. Mixed in among them were shield-bearers whose sole responsibility was to carry large tower shields with a spike on the bottom that could be driven into the ground. The shield-bearers and pike wielders could then take cover behind them.

Further behind marched row after row of infantry dressed in lightweight armor of leather and chainmail. Some carried only swords, while others carried a sword and a small buckler shield, and yet others carried less conventional weapons such as whips and daggers. They weren't the typical weapons of battle, but in the hands of specialists, they could be used to devastating effect. Then bringing up the rear were dozens and dozens of skilled archers with longbows, short bows, and crossbows, all ready to rain arrows and bolts down on their enemies.

Not a single soldier from the Narsdin region remained in Kern once the group had fully exited the city gates. In fact, even a few of the city's residents fashioned homemade weapons from farming tools or other bits and pieces found laying around the city and now followed behind the smaller army. They vowed their loyalty to the one they felt had released them from Lord Shiron's oppression. The soldiers attempted to dissuade the peasants from following due to their lack of training, armor, and real weapons, but their efforts were half-hearted at best since their main priority was hurrying to their master's aid. There were those who felt it quicker and easier just to shoot their followers with arrows, but others argued that those arrows could be better used on the enemy ahead. Others were perfectly fine with sacrificing the pitiful citizens who followed them.

"Better them than us," one of the soldiers even remarked to another, insinuating that he would rather see the people of Kern be used as shields and die so that he and his comrades may live to continue the fight.

The real problem this group faced though was not the would-be soldiers who followed them but the lack of information about their master's current whereabouts or direction of travel. The group was made up of skilled fighters across many disciplines, but they lacked anyone who could effectively track the other army's progress. All they had to go on was what little information their informant had been able to glean from Lord Veyron.

They knew only that their leader had headed west and nothing more. Did they turn west from Rhorm? From Mechii? From somewhere else? They had no idea how far south they needed to go before turning west to follow in the footsteps of their master. Their only option was to march south first and look for signs that may point in the direction of their fellow soldiers so that their army could be made whole again.

Chapter 6

Riorik hurried the others that came with him along towards his friend and

destiny. Even if he didn't have magical greaves granting him increased

agility and stamina, the young elf would still be moving faster than he ever

had before. He pushed on, determined to cover the ground between him

and Nordahs as quickly as he could manage. Every second that passed

filled the young elf's mind with thoughts of arriving too late and finding his friend bloodied and dead on the ground. His mind flashed back to the oasis, and it replayed Wuffred's demise, occasionally substituting Wuffred's face with Nordahs'. Such thoughts and worries pushed the elf to run faster, take bigger strides, and carry on no matter what.

Eventually, the young Ranger looked behind him and realized that in his fear he'd not only left the gnomes and dwarves behind but the humans and barbarians. Even with their longer legs, they were also struggling to keep up with the racing elf. Riorik was left with no choice but to slow down so that the others could better keep up.

Luckily for Riorik, it didn't take long for him to pick up the trail of his friend, and the trail was fresh. This encouraged Riorik at first. Nordahs was obviously still moving and alive. But after additional scrutiny of his friend's tracks, Riorik's sense of excitement and relief was replaced by concern. The tracks of his friend showed a much slower pace than Riorik had expected. And there were other tracks only slightly older that surrounded the tracks Nordahs had left behind.

Riorik's mind began to race anew with thoughts of his friend's capture. The young elf began to panic, but then he saw the truth of the situation in the tracks. Riorik could see the large depressions made by the assortment of fleeing orcs and trolls. Then, Riorik reexamined the other tracks that surrounded Nordahs' tracks. These were older than Nordahs' and looked to be made by humans moving very slowly, as if they'd been tracking or following the horde while hiding their presence. The tracks were more defined than any tracks a trained Ranger, elven or otherwise, would ever make, but there was no mistaking their attempts at disguising their tracks and hiding their numbers. It was all classic stalking techniques that Riorik quickly picked up on. And then, on top of those tracks, Riorik found the faint markings of his elven friend, a task that only another elf or an expert tracker would've been able to do.

Having detected the second group's attempts at stealth, Riorik felt reassured once more that Nordahs hadn't been captured and was doing well. The details implied that Nordahs was following the humans who were tracking the horde toward Brennan to the west. All that was left for

Riorik now was to follow Nordahs, and his friend would lead him to both.

Whether or not that would be a good thing was something only time

would tell, but that did little to deter Riorik, who was still anxious to be

reunited with his friend.

Satisfied that Nordahs was nearby based on the freshness of the tracks,

Riorik pushed on. Those who'd managed to catch up with Riorik were

curious about what the tracks had revealed to the elf, but Riorik only

answered, "they're near."

But as the elf continued forward, the latest threat still loomed overhead. It

was approaching midday now, and the light that filled the openness of the

plains offered little in terms of protection and camouflage to Riorik and his

new allies. As they drew nearer and nearer to the horde's position, they

could be more easily spotted by any scouts or the lookouts who were

almost certainly watching for them. All Riorik could do was continue on, hoping that Nordahs had come to the same conclusion and that his tracks would lead them to safety rather than danger.

#

The horses and riders under Lord Veyron's command rode ahead at full gallop. Lord Veyron wanted the faster units to not only scout ahead to find the fastest, if not necessarily the safest, place that his troops could cross the river, but to also make sure that their opponents hadn't turned north towards Tyleco. The middle-aged Lord was confident that the thick, sturdy walls that encircled his town could withstand any assault the horde could manage, but he was unsure just what else the legendary breastplate could do. He'd seen it take a lance at full charge and reduce it to splinters, so for all he knew, the breastplate could topple towers and walls upon command. Lord Veyron was not interested in seeing his city reduced to rubble by the power of the armor, but rather possess that power for himself to use, should it be needed, in his quest for the throne. This meant reaching the armor's current owner as quickly as possible, even if it meant putting some of his men at greater risk than necessary.

Compared to Riorik and his allies, Lord Veyron could cover much more ground than the elf. His horses were well conditioned and well-fed, allowing them to gallop for long periods and cover a lot of territory. The downside to this rapid pace was the level of exhaustion that was setting in among those chasing behind on foot. No matter how well one is trained or how good their stamina is, no human would ever be able to match the speed of a good horse—not that Lord Veyron concerned himself with such thoughts. His mind was focused on the armor he knew to be in Ammudien's possession and adorned by his latest enemy. Driven by greed, desire, and lust, Lord Veyron was only concerned with getting the armor for his own selfish purposes, regardless of what that cost him or the men who struggled to keep up with his torturous pace.

In a short time, the knights reached the river, identified what they thought would be the fastest point to cross without deviating the army's path significantly, and returned to relay their findings to their leader. Lord

Veyron immediately adjusted course to march directly to the crossing

point before spurring his horse to a full gallop in that direction. The hooves

of the horses flung clumps of grass and dirt into the air as they raced off

towards the river. The other troops were left to follow as quickly as their

legs could carry them, something the more heavily armored units

struggled with even at slower paces.

Several minutes later, the group successfully traversed the same distance

that had taken Riorik and his friends the better part of a day to cross and

arrived at the river's northern bank. Lord Veyron remained seated in his

saddle while he surveyed the river's flowing waters and the muddy shore

on the opposite side. In his mind, the river marked the last obstacle that

stood between him and the armor that would make him king. Without

hesitation, he ordered his knights to cross on their horses and await

further orders. The horses crossed the waters with relative ease, the water

barely reaching their knees as the river flowed at a manageable speed, unlike the raging currents nearer to the waterfalls where the river split. Now all that was left was to wait for the slower troops to arrive so that they could cross too.

Eventually, the regular soldiers arrived. Many of them groaned at the thought of trying to drag their weary bodies across the river. Their legs were exhausted from trying to keep pace with the knights, and many of them were afraid they lacked the strength to make the crossing.

Lord Veyron was annoyed at the moaning and complaining that arose from the group, but he eventually came to understand and even appreciate their position. Regardless, the determined lord would not be denied or delayed by a few naysayers among his ranks. He ordered a few of his archers to fire arrows with ropes attached to them into several of the trees on the opposite riverbank before tying them off around the trunks. The idea was that the troops could hold on to the ropes as they crossed, so even if their tired legs gave out, they wouldn't be swept downriver by the current.

It wasn't the response that many of them had hoped for from their esteemed leader, but it was an order that they were expected to follow, and follow they did. The archers embedded about half a dozen lines in the trees along the riverbank before securing their ends on other nearby trees. One by one, the troops formed lines behind each rope and trotted off across the river. Some found the water's cold temperature refreshing while others shrieked and shrilled at the sudden change.

Lord Veyron remained to help encourage and direct the flow of soldiers across to the other side. His urge was to ride on and leave this task to his other knights, but he knew the wisest course of action was to remain with his troops. The task of organizing his soldiers to get them across the river as efficiently as possible served as a much-needed distraction for the green-eyed leader of men. It helped to keep his mind from obsessing on the armor and its potential to boost his chances of becoming king.

It took several minutes for the soldiers to complete the crossing, but they did all eventually manage to make it safely to the other side. There were a few soldiers who slipped on the rocky, uneven riverbed, but they were quickly caught and steadied by their comrades. There was a close call when one soldier lost his footing and fell into the water. Unable to grab on to anything in his panic, the water pushed the man downriver, but fortunately he became entangled in the legs of other soldiers crossing on another line.

Satisfied that his men had crossed the river, Lord Veyron encouraged them to continue their march. But before the conglomerate of soldiers could move, one of Lord Veyron's knights decided to speak up in opposition to his leader's rushed attitude.

"Sire," the knight started, "perhaps it would be prudent to give the men a moment to wring out their clothing before we move on."

The knight pointed to several soldiers who had taken to wringing out their tunics, pants, and even long johns, desperate to dry their clothes as much as possible. Those who wore the heavier armors, which included boots, were busy trying to drain water out from their protective metallic casings.

The knight's objection to Veyron's command vexed the leader, who was not accustomed to having his troops question his orders. But as he looked around and took into consideration the impact such an order would have, Lord Veyron began to think better of his decision.

"Very well," he replied to the knight before turning to address his army as a whole.

"Soldiers of Tyleco," he began, "our fight draws near. It has been a demanding and tiring effort to reach this place, I know. Before we continue on to our destiny and the salvation of our homes, let us take a few moments to gather our thoughts, dry our clothes, and regain our strength. Unfortunately, destiny does not wait long, so do these things quickly, and be sure to do them while you can."

A collective sigh could be heard from the scattered members of the group. Many of them were relieved to know that they wouldn't be expected to immediately chase after the horses again. But Lord Veyron had ulterior motives for his decision. He put a political spin on his words to try and assuage any resentment or anger that his recent actions may have caused

his men, but Lord Veyron wanted the men to be refreshed for battle in his

name, and he knew that waterlogged soldiers would move slower and

louder than he wanted. Lord Veyron didn't want his army's approach to be

signalled to his opponent by the sounds of sloshing and squishing water.

The wait would cost him precious minutes in his hunt for the armor but

would grant him invaluable extra effort from his soldiers and a tactical

advantage that he would otherwise lack.

#

"I seek to form a bond, an alliance, with the bandit king," the armored elf

declared as soon as the two leaders had taken seat across from one

another in the now empty dining hall.

The long table stretched the length of the room, obviously designed to

accommodate dozens of people. Two other tables of similar length sat on

either side of the room, but the two leaders chose to be seated at the

center table for their talks.

"Straight to business I see," countered Draynard. "Perhaps you are more like me than I first gave you credit for."

"I fail to see the similarities," huffed the elf, "but regardless, would you like to hear my offer?"

"By all means," answered Draynard. He leaned back in his chair and folded his arms across his chest.

The bandit king's expression was one of blank curiosity. He was well versed in such conversations and had learned to not give away his thoughts or reactions, even in his facial expressions. With a single cocked eyebrow, King Draynard was ready to listen, but little else was apparent by looking at him.

"I am here to make you an offer in return for an alliance and—"

"So, you've said," interrupted Draynard. "I know what you expect from me in return, but the question remains, what is it you offer me in exchange for that alliance and protection?"

"What is it that you seek?" asked the masked elf. "Name your price."

Draynard instantly recognized the classic negotiating technique. Being the skilled and experienced bandit, Draynard was not foolish enough to fall for such a simple and obvious ploy. He decided to play a game with his guest. After all, he wasn't in a rush to secure this alliance. Rather, it was the other way around.

"Oh, that could be something quite substantial. A price I'm not sure that you can meet," Draynard initially answered.

"Why don't you make me an offer, and then we can see what kind of an arrangement we might reach," the elf quickly countered.

This was not the type of negotiation the elven king desired. He had hoped that Draynard would just give him a price that he could agree to and then move on. Oddly enough though, the elf hadn't brought any money with him when he left Macadre. He had always intended to loot the towns that he conquered along the way, so even if Draynard gave him a price, he would be unable to immediately pay the bandit in full.

"I can offer you any amount of gold and riches that you desire," the crafty elf continued in the hope that Draynard, tempted by the promises of riches, would throw out a number finally.

"And where are these gold and riches that you offer?" questioned Draynard. "Or have you forgotten that my men and I followed you here to the gates of my city? Your men carried no chests. Your caravan did not include any wagons or carts filled with plundered goods. Unless you plan to pay me with the trinkets stashed in your pockets, which would be an insult by the way, I don't know that you have the ability to make good on such an offer."

The realization that Draynard was equally aware of his empty coffers was annoying to the desperate elf. He decided a slightly different approach might be in order.

"You are wise and with keen eyes to notice such shortcomings. It is true that I come to you with empty pockets offering only promises and not real coin. My wealth remains in Macadre where my coffers bulge with coin, ample enough to satisfy any desires one such as yourself may entertain. If you are open to agreeing to receive your payment later, then I can arrange to have whatever amount you seek delivered. I will see that a messenger bird is dispatched this moment if you so desire."

The elven king then paused for a moment before continuing.

"But I think I can offer you something more than a few shiny coins and sparkling baubles. I think that we share similar ambitions, and together, we can see both of our dreams comes to fruition. How does that sound? Does that not interest you?"

Draynard spotted the dark king's pitiful attempt to try and trick the bandit king into revealing his own ambitions.

"And what ambitions would those be?" the bandit king responded. "All things living have ambitions, even the smallest creatures have ambitions of eating and surviving. The fact that we each have ambitions towards self-preservation is not enough to say that we are alike. Or are our ambitions so similar that an alliance should be formed on that basis alone? You will need to speak more directly if you want me, a simple bandit, to truly

understand your meaning."

And even though Draynard's thoughts filled with sarcasm and contempt

for his guest's attempts to goad him into making the first offer, something

no respectable bandit would ever consider doing, the skillful bandit

managed to maintain a straight face and speak with a calm tone. The

bandit king refused to reveal his true emotions still.

The bandit's unwillingness to disadvantage himself by the elf's prompting

was becoming more and more annoying to the elven king. He'd expected

the bandit leader to be little more than a greedy coin chaser who would

sell his loyalty to the highest bidder. But once more, it seemed that the elf

from Narsdin had underestimated another of his opponents. Frustrated,

he opted to stop the games and just cut right to the chase.

"Let us stop pretending," the annoyed elf started. "You and I both know

that you have, plainly speaking, ambitions to rule more than just this

town. Just as I have ambitions to rule more than just the desolate and isolated northern region. We both strive for greatness and think we can offer more if only we had more authority. You and I have both been overshadowed by those around us for far too long, and now it is our time to rise to the top. But, sadly, neither of us can make that ascent on our own. We need each other so that we may each reach our true potential. That is my true offer."

The bandit took a deep breath as he thought about the elf's words and how best to respond. His offer was concerning to the bandit, but at the same time, it was intriguing.

"So, let me get this straight," Draynard replied after several seconds of contemplation. "You pledge to support me in my claim for the throne, granting me authority over the humans of Corsallis in exchange for me and my men helping you to slaughter and oppress the other peoples of this same land? So, in other words, I help you kill thousands and you help me translate that genocidal act into getting the approval of my people to name me king. Do I have that right?"

The elf could only chuckle at Draynard's negativity and sarcasm. But it didn't take a maniacal and ruthless invader to put a political spin on the bandit's words.

"You could look at it that way, yes. But I would say that you should rather view it like this: if you help me remove those who would otherwise object to my effort to make Corsallis better , I will help you to remove any obstacles preventing you from sitting on the human throne. I found that in Narsdin, people will follow their leader regardless of how they've obtained power if they have something to fear from it. If your people think you are weak, then they will work to oppose or depose your authority. Whereas, if they think you are strong and have strong alliances, then the risks for them are too great and they will go along with your rule rather than jeopardize what little self-worth they feel they have."

"Ruling is never easy, this is something you need to understand if you are to be the king. There are those that call me an oppressor because I do not give my people total freedom, but I have seen what freedom can do to societies and have found that a stricter rule can prove more fruitful and be easier to maintain. I do not oppress the people of Narsdin, but rather, I give them stricter guidelines for them to live their lives within for the benefit of all who dwell there. Sure, those who speak out against me have received harsh punishments but that is to ensure that the number of dissenters is kept low, thus allowing me to focus on how to continue my beneficial reign. If I spent all of my time fighting to retain power, then my lands would break apart into the same segregated regions that have prevented many of you from reaching your true potential. It is about focus, and I keep my focus on what lies ahead by making sure that I don't have to focus on who is approaching from behind."

It was the most real thing the elf had said since the two had started this conversation, but somehow, it still didn't feel completely sincere to the bandit. Draynard still had concerns about the unknown invader, and like any good bandit, felt the whole thing smelled of treachery. There were no guarantees that Draynard could ask for to make him believe that the elf wouldn't kill him and claim the human throne for himself the moment the elf no longer needed his help. Why would Draynard believe that this outsider's goal was to rule everyone in Corsallis except the humans? That would make Draynard a source of competition or opposition later. The elf's offer was certainly tempting, but the risk to the bandit still seemed exceptionally great.

"That is an interesting offer, when you put it like that," Draynard finally replied. "It is an offer that I must consider carefully and not make a rash decision about. Surely you understand?"

"I can understand your need to consider things, but time is of the essence, let's not forget, so I would urge you not to take too long in your consideration," the elf answered.

Chapter 7

Once across the river, it didn't take Lord Veyron and his men long to zero

in on the horde's current location. Still waiting outside the gates of

Brennan, the horde had broken into smaller groups, lighting small fires to

warm themselves in the fading light and heat up what food stocks

remained. Trails of smoke billowed high into the sky, acting as beacons to

the trained human soldiers who were familiar with Brennan's environs and the typical activity surrounding the bandit town. The additional smoke could only mean one thing—an increase in Brennan's population. With the infantry still trailing behind, the knights made directly for Brennan.

The ride was a short one, taking a slightly southwesterly course from where they'd just crossed the river. The River Via flowed from the west to the east, with a bifurcation that created the River Freca distributary. Brennan was situated near the River Freca, the southernmost river of the two distributaries, which emptied into Lake Morthia. The forces from Tyleco could ride and march along the river's western shores and arrive directly at the city, where the horde was now believed to have made camp.

This was good news for the marching humans for a few reasons. First, they now had access to an endless supply of fresh water. Second, the river also provided access to fresh food, such as fish, turtles, frogs, and other animals that took sustenance from the river. Third, the river created a natural barrier that would slow the horde's advancement west and create an opportunity to inflict significant damage on them if they were caught attempting to cross the river. And lastly, the moist soil that lined the river was flush with trees, bushes, and tall grasses that would provide many of Lord Veyron's troops ample cover as they drew nearer the horde, allowing the humans the element of surprise.

The only thing Lord Veyron didn't know was what exactly was the horde doing at Brennan. He didn't know if they were attempting to capture Brennan as they had Kern—a thought that was not completely repellant to Veyron, since that would likely remove another of his rivals for the throne. More frightening to Lord Veyron was the possibility that the horde had joined forces with the bandits of Brennan and now their two armies were one. His attack on the horde would be more difficult, but bandits weren't known for their mettle in all-out battle and were more adept at fighting from the shadows or against defenseless travelers. Lord Veyron still liked his army's odds, even if his enemy had the bandit's help. His ambition convinced him it would be worth the risk, especially with the chance of

taking the legendary breastplate for himself.

And so he pressed on, even though he didn't know exactly what he and his

men would face at Brennan.

#

Riorik continued following the various tracks left by those who'd preceded

him, but the tracks of greatest importance to the elf were those left by his

friend Nordahs. Nordahs' tracks remained imprinted atop the others and

therefore were the freshest among all that Riorik found, which was a good

sign. With every track Riorik found showing his friend as the most recent

to pass by, he became more confident that a joyful reunion with his friend

was imminent.

But just as Riorik had all but pushed the last of the dread about his friend's

untimely demise from his mind, Nordahs' tracks ended. The elf's footprints

stopped suddenly and without expectation, and Riorik looked around

feverishly for clues. The ground showed no signs of a struggle, of another party intersecting with Nordahs, or any indication that Nordahs had changed direction. It was as if the elf was there one minute and then gone the next.

And just like that, all Riorik's thoughts of happily reuniting with his friend were replaced once more with visions of him finding his friend's mangled corpse.

Careful not to disturb the tracks that may hold information about his friend's whereabouts, Riorik swung his head from side to side looking for clues. He was so focused on looking for signs of Nordahs' movements that the elf was completely taken by surprise when a hand shot out of some nearby bushes and grabbed his arm.

Riorik squealed in shock before another hand flew out from the leafy vegetation and covered his mouth, muffling the elf's high-pitched yell. Yanked behind the bushes, Riorik was filled with joy and relief to see that the hands in question belonged to Nordahs, except Nordahs didn't look as happy to see Riorik as he did to see Nordahs.

"What's wrong with you?" Nordahs asked in a hushed but still somewhat angry tone. "I thought they'd trained us better than that."

He stared at his still stunned friend and shook his head in disbelief at Riorik's reaction.

"Bandits were following your father's army. I had to hide here to avoid being seen," Nordahs whispered to Riorik, knowing what was bound to be his friend's first question once he'd regained the ability to speak again.

"There are others following me," Riorik whispered loudly in response.

Nordahs hushed his friend again for still making too much noise.

"Go back and let them know," Nordahs encouraged Riorik. "I won't go anywhere until you get back, but you need to warn them to stop here before anyone sees them."

"But if it's only some bandits, don't you think after what they did at Mechii, they could handle it?"

Nordahs sighed in frustration at his friend's lack of trust.

"It's not that. I think the bandits may be working with your father," Nordahs countered, still talking in hushed tones. "I saw your father enter the city with someone who claimed to be the leader of the bandits. They didn't fight one another. Instead, they talked and then walked off together. If the bandits spot our new friends, then we may face a bigger force than anticipated before we're ready. You need to go stop their advance and find a way to discreetly lead them here so we can stay out of view while we figure out how to proceed."

"Makes sense," is all Riorik had to say in reply.

He poked his head back out of the bushes and looked around to make sure the area was still clear. Convinced he could leave the same way he came without being seen, Riorik followed the trail back to where the others stopped when they'd lost sight of Riorik. The Ranger explained the situation to the barbarians and Rory before quietly leading them to Nordahs' hiding spot.

"I've got to go back and get the gnomes and dwarves now," Riorik told his friend. "They couldn't keep up with our longer strides. If I don't go back for them, they'll walk straight into Father's army."

Nordahs nodded in agreement, and once more Riorik disappeared through the bushes and into the open fields.

The gnomes and dwarves were moving at a fast pace considering their size, but it still took Riorik several minutes to cover the gap between the two positions. Again, he explained Nordahs' recent discovery of a possible alliance between the horde and the bandits. He explained that Nordahs had managed to find a protected spot nearby that they could hide in until they decided what their next move would be.

For the third time, Riorik followed the tracks, only this time a bit slower than before, back to where Nordahs had jumped off the path and into hiding.

Riorik kept watch as he directed the seemingly endless line of gnomes and dwarves through the bushes and into the increasingly cramped space where Nordahs had hidden. The space was little more than a barren patch of dirt hidden among a few large weeping willow trees and leafy bushes, but it was enough to obscure the group from the view of any passersby. Once everyone had managed to squeeze into the hiding spot, Riorik made his way through the crowd towards his friend, who was now reunited with Ammudien, Rory, and Kirin.

"Do you mages know a spell to muffle the sounds of our voices to keep them from carrying across the winds?" Riorik quietly asked Ammudien.

"I do not, but I know someone who does," Ammudien whispered back.

"That's from the school of wind, not terra, so I need to find someone familiar with that discipline."

The small gnome slipped away into the throng of people for only a minute before returning.

"Done," he said, no longer whispering.

"Are you sure? I didn't notice anything," a concerned Riorik said, still whispering.

"Do you always see when I cast spells, or do you always see what my spells produce?" countered the gnome. "This isn't a fireball spell or anything that would yield a visible effect, but I assure you, it's been taken care of."

"Now that we may talk freely," started Nordahs, "we need to figure out what to do about these two groups. I think they may be working together but have nothing to support that theory other than seeing the leaders talking to one another at one point."

"On the contrary, I have to assume there isn't an alliance between the two groups," countered Rory. "If the army of our own allies marched to Tyleco, then we would've undoubtedly grant them access to our city. We wouldn't leave our allies locked out of the city where they'd be more vulnerable to attack. They wouldn't have access to smiths to repair or improve their armaments, not to mention access to food for their troops. The bandit king leaving them outside the city like this doesn't look like an alliance to me."

"Then what do you think is happening?" asked Nordahs, curious to understand how his assessment was wrong.

"You said you saw the two talking, right?" asked Rory.

"Yes, that's correct," answered Nordahs.

"As a military man myself, there are two obvious reasons why the leaders of two different forces would talk under these circumstances. One would be to negotiate some type of alliance or truce to gain supplies or resources one group needs from the other. Considering the losses suffered at Mechii, it's plausible that he's looking to barter with the bandits for weapons, supplies, and possibly mercenaries."

"And the second reason?" a curious Riorik asked his friend before he could continue his thought.

"The second," Rory continued, giving Riorik an annoyed look for the interruption, "is that your father's trying to negotiate a surrender. It would explain why his troops remain outside the city. The bandits could've confronted them but found themselves unprepared for the size of his army, so your father gave the bandits an option to surrender or have their homes besieged. They could've gone inside together to discuss the terms of surrender and the transfer of leadership, with your father's troops staying outside as a reminder of his power and as a threat if something happened to him while in the city."

"So, militarily speaking, you think the two groups are not in alignment against us, but may either be trading goods or one is consuming the other?" Ammudien asked Rory, just to make sure he'd followed the human's thoughts properly.

"Yeah," Rory responded simply, confirming Ammudien's summary.

"But wait," Riorik interrupted again. "Does this mean that if we attack my father's forces outside of Brennan that the bandits will do nothing, or will they help us, or help them? I'm still confused."

Nordahs shook his head in dismay at his friend's dimwittedness but was careful to not let Riorik see. Rory had Riorik's attention, answering the elf's rather obvious question.

"The simple answer is that we don't know," Rory replied to Riorik. "If the bandits are negotiating their own surrender, then there's a good chance they'd take the opportunity to fight against their would-be occupiers. Even if they don't fight with us, they would fight our common enemy. But if they're brokering a trade agreement to provide supplies to your father's men, then there's a good chance they'd either do nothing or fight against us for disrupting their profiteering.

"And then we still must consider Nordahs' theory of the two groups forming an alliance, as we have with the dwarves, gnomes, and barbarians. If they are, then we'd be up against both forces together. I mean, it's hard to say which scenario is more likely because we don't really know enough about what's going on inside the city. All we know is that the northern forces are camped out here while your father is inside the city gates, presumably with the leader of the bandits. That's not really enough to say with any certainty what we're dealing with here."

"I could always use my invisibility spell to eavesdrop on the army encamped outside the gates or maybe get into the city to see if I can learn what else is going on," Ammudien suggested to the group.

"No, it might take too long to gain any actionable intelligence. Plus, that puts you in great danger walking among them alone," Riorik said, shooting down the gnome's idea.

"What else would you have us do?" Nordahs asked his friend. "It's not like we're bursting with ideas, and we have no idea how long it may be before we learn which of our theories are correct. For all we know, your father may be sending a message back to wherever he found this army to send more help. I don't think waiting is a sensible option at this point."

Riorik had to admit that Nordahs was right, they couldn't afford to just sit around and wait to see what would happen next. They risked the horde regaining its strength, either by bolstering its numbers, improving its gear, or even more frightening, doing both.

They had an army too. An army made up of powerful mages, strong

barbarians, and stout dwarves carrying blunderbusses that in many cases

could even the odds. Riorik only had to give the word and the assault

would begin. But the young elf struggled with the decision that could

potentially cost so many their lives. He was torn, not eager to be the one

to make that call.

#

The knights of Tyleco slowed their horses to a walk as they neared their

destination, just outside Brennan where the stacks of smoke continued to

rise. They wanted to keep the movements of their horses as quiet as

possible, and slowing down also reduced the jingle jangle of the riders'

armor. Following behind them, the infantry now had a chance to catch up

to the faster cavalry units.

With the full force of Tyleco's army gathered, Lord Veyron sent a couple of

his light-footed archers to get a better look. The troops were still a safe

distance from the city's walls, but it was apparent to Veyron's scouts that the men acting as lookouts in Brennan were aware of their approach. The scouts could see three men on top of the city's outer wall, pointing in the direction that the archers had just come from. The scouts watched as others appeared next to the lookouts on the wall and were directed to look at the same area.

As Veyron's scouts sat and watched, they came to realize that although their approach had been seen, the bandit lookouts had now lost track of them. The scouts were safe to move about as long as they remained stealthy. There was no sign from atop the wall that the bandits were interested in sending anyone out to investigate what they'd seen.

It was perfect for Lord Veyron and his men, only they had no way of knowing the lookouts were so easily fooled.

Meanwhile, the archers used any cover they could find to make their way nearer the rising smoke—trees, bushes, large rocks, abandoned huts, crumbling fences, and in one case, even hiding behind a lone cow roaming the fields. The scouts circled the area, viewing the horde from a variety of angles to gather as much information as they could.

They found the horde in various activities. Some were eating, some sleeping, some sharpening their blades, and others appeared to be passing the time gambling with dice. The horde had let its guard down. If there were ever a time to attack, it was now. The scouts hurried back to Lord Veyron, eager to pass on what they'd seen.

"So they are unprepared," Lord Veyron said aloud to himself.

He was happy to hear that the army was little more than sitting ducks. But there was one more detail the scouts had not yet reported on.

"And what about the one with the shiny green breastplate? Where was he and what was he doing?" Lord Veyron asked them as he tried to hold back his impatience.

"We didn't see anyone with such a breastplate. Most of the troops wore little armor, and even fewer had a breastplate of any color. We saw no one with green armor."

The response was a setback for the anxious leader. But he immediately knew what that must mean.

"Then he's inside the city and we must draw him out," Lord Veyron said. He pulled on the reins of his horse and turned to face his knights and commanders, who'd gathered around to hear the scouts' report with him. "Attack and attack now. Show those vile beasts no mercy and be sure to be as loud as possible in the process," he ordered them.

The first order was typical for the seasoned soldiers, but the part about being loud seemed a little strange. Strange enough that one of the knights sought clarification from his leader.

"Pardon me, my liege, but did you say to be loud when we attacked them?" the knight asked cautiously.

Lord Veyron scowled at the knight, annoyed at having to explain his command, but he answered the question as calmly as he could manage. "Yes, be loud," began Lord Veyron's reply. "If their leader is within the city, then we need to make noise to draw him out. If you don't make a scene, he'll have no reason to leave the safety of the city and then I won't be able to kill him and take his breastplate."

The mention of the breastplate he so desperately wanted instantly reminded Lord Veyron that he hadn't given any orders for how his men were to approach the masked king.

"When the elf with the green breastplate appears, nobody is to attack him. He is mine to kill. And what he bears is mine to collect. Any of your men who fail to heed this order will be considered a traitor and put to death on the spot. Make sure that everyone understands this."

It was a most unusual order from Lord Veyron. He was not typically eager to ride into battle himself and often let his troops loot whatever goods they could find from their downed foes. For him to single out an enemy, especially one known to be possessive enormous strength, was most unlike their leader, but regardless, it was his order and they were to comply.

"How soon would you have us attack?" another of the knights then asked.

Lord Veyron's reply was short and definitive. "Now!"

The men scurried away to pass on their lord's orders and begin the attack.

The foot soldiers were led by the scouts to where they'd observed the horde earlier. Luckily for them, the lookouts atop the walls of Brennan had moved on, leaving a large gap in the city's watch and allowing the Tyleco's men to easily move into position. Their orders were to wait there for the knights' charge, and when the knights attacked, to rush in behind the cavalry.

It only took a few minutes after Lord Veyron gave his command for the well-disciplined soldiers to get into position. Once the knights received the ready signal from the scouts, they kicked their horses into a full gallop and charged ahead.

The horses leaped together over a row of shrubs that separated them from the horde and charged at full gallop into the view of the unsuspecting army. By the time the sound of the horses' hooves could be heard over the chatter of the horde, it was too late.

The knights led the attack, impaling as many of their foes as they could before the lances broke. They focused on the larger orcs and trolls and were able to take down a few, but the element of surprise didn't last long. A few of the knights were taken out by their intended targets.

As one knight made his fateful charge at a nearby troll, the hulking beast stood up and readied itself against the knight's attack. The knight thrust his lance towards the troll when his horse drew close, but his strike missed. The slow, clumsy troll somehow managed to sidestep the attack before reaching out and grabbing the knight's lance. The knight was so stunned by the turn of events that he held fast to the lance as his horse continued to run forward.

The troll's grip was far stronger than the knight's grip on his horse's saddle, so the troll easily yanked the knight from his mount. He hit the ground with a solid thud, and between the weight of his armor and the disorientation of impact, the knight was slow to right himself.

The troll took one step, hovering directly above the knight. The lance was still firmly in the troll's grip. The knight had no chance of defending himself from what came next. The troll used its trunk-like leg and monstrous foot to kick the knight in the head as he tried to pull himself to his feet. The kick sent the knight back down to the ground with another hard impact, leaving him completely defenseless.

The troll then took the knight's own lance and drove it into his helm. The impact was brutal. The lance broke apart but not before the lance's metal tip crushed the knight's visor so deep into the knight's face that it nearly sliced the man's nose clean from his face.

The knight cried out in agony, muffled by a steady stream of blood gushing from the area. He gurgled as the blood filled his mouth. Dissatisfied with the weakness of the lance and its inability to finish the job, the troll tossed what remained of the weapon aside and decided to use its own foot to do what the lance could not.

The troll stomped several times on the knight's head as hard as it could. With each blow, the damaged helmet crushed further into the knight's skull. Blood spurted from inside the once shiny plate. The knight had stopped screaming after the first stomp, but the troll was determined to make sure he was dead. The troll didn't stop until the helmet had been squashed nearly flat, stomping with such violence that the troll failed to notice the knight's head had detached from the rest of his body so that in the end, the troll was only crushing a decapitated head.

Lord Veyron, meanwhile, had ridden his horse to the center of the horde's camp. He used his trusty sword to swat away anyone who approached his position, but for the most part, his troops were doing a good job of attacking the disorganized horde, preventing them from regrouping or reaching the center of camp where Veyron was located. He wanted to stay away from the action but not because he didn't want to fight—he wanted to be certain he could see when the breastplate-wearing soldier returned to the field.

Lord Veyron watched his men yelling and screaming as they fought the horde. His archers let out battle cries when launching volleys of arrows into the battlefield. Occasionally, their arrows struck some of their less-armored cohorts, much to the archers' chagrin.

His knights continued darting in and out of battle on their horses, or at least those who hadn't been unseated by their foes. The knights on the ground were forced to ditch their now-unwieldy lances in exchange for the steel longswords that hung from their belts.

The other infantrymen were forced to chose their targets carefully, as they wore thinner armor and carried less robust weapons. None of the infantrymen dared attack the orcs and trolls. Instead, they opted to leave those powerful enemies for the better-armed knights to test their skills against.

Through it all, Lord Veyron remained unmoved from his position. He watched his men but always kept a close eye on Brennan's gate, watching for when his true target appeared.

"The bandits do not aide the horde but rather watch their slaughter," Lord Veyron thought to himself and tried to work out why in his head.

But before he could find a rational reason for the bandits' lack of action, Lord Veyron's thoughts were interrupted and his attention drawn to the creaking sounds of the city's gate being hauled open.

Chapter 8

The noise of Lord Veyron's ambush on the horde had not gone unnoticed.

The two leaders sat safely around the table while Draynard contemplated

the elf's offer in total silence. He remained conflicted. The offer of help to

secure the crown sounded good, but the ever-present threat of his ally

later turning on him prevented the human from allying with the elf. The

sounds of fighting were a happy distraction for the bandit.

And while the lookouts on the city's wall seemed to take no action in the fighting that raged outside the city, the city's guards were sure to make this recent development known to their leader. The sounds of fighting created a rather tense moment between the two leaders. They initially accused each other of attacking their people, and while both leaders vehemently denied being responsible for the fighting, neither of them truly believed the other. The stand-off was quickly ended when one of Draynard's men burst through the doors of the dining hall and informed the two rulers of the situation.

"An army carrying the flag of Tyleco surprise attacked the army camped outside out walls. They have horses, bowmen, and infantry. They caught the troops unprepared. It is a slaughter!" the guard exclaimed, the words erupting from his mouth before he could think better of it.

The elf slammed his hands down on the table and pushed himself back and up from his seated position. He said nothing to either man standing in the room but cast a look of suspicion in Draynard's direction. He quickly

stormed out of the room and moved towards the city's gate.

Draynard followed behind his guest but stopped in front of the guard who

reported the attack.

"What should we do, King Draynard? Do we help the stranger or Lord

Veyron?" the guard asked cautiously, obviously confused about where

their loyalty lied.

"We do nothing," Draynard casually replied. "The stranger has yet to offer

me anything of value in exchange for our support, and Lord Veyron

believes that he is better than us, so we would only be in his way. If he

wants to fight this fight, then we will let him. It is not any business of ours,

at least not yet."

"And what if Lord Veyron should attack the city?" the guard asked next.

"If he is foolish enough to attack us when we've done nothing to him, then

it will be a declaration of war, and we will have no choice but to defend

ourselves and end his pitiful rule," Draynard replied without even pausing to think about it. Apparently, it was something the bandit king had been mentally prepared for.

Draynard resumed walking to the gate. His guard followed closely behind.

#

The large wooden gates of Brennan swung open with the help of several nearby bandits. As the gates swung fully open, the elf in the shiny green breastplate stood in the middle of the gate's frame. And, for the first time in Lord Veyron's presence, held the similarly shiny green sword in his hand, ready to fight. The armored elf hadn't forgotten the effect he'd had on the Tyleco knights when his armor took the brute force of a charging knight's lance and brushed it aside like one would an insect. Now, he was ready to make another display of his power.

Draynard looked on from a distance, curious about the odd-looking sword that obviously matched the equally odd-looking breastplate the elf wore. Earlier, the bandit leader, who had no idea about the breastplate's true identity, just assumed it was part of a collection of random bits used to create a full suit of armor for the horde's leader or perhaps a trophy taken from another foe in a distant land. But now, Draynard began to doubt his previous assumption and looked at the matching items with renewed interest.

Meanwhile, the Macadrian king locked eyes with the mounted Lord Veyron in the center of the fight. Lord Veyron looked at the breastplate with lust in his eyes and drool in his mouth. That is, until he noticed the matching sword. It didn't take long for Raiken's descendent to recognize the legendary sword from the stories told to him as a child. This filled the mounted lord with both fear and rage simultaneously. The fear came from the realization that his foe not only possessed Trylon's Ascension Armor breastplate, but also Raiken's Ascension Armor sword. One piece of the armor made his enemy very formidable, but two pieces made him nearly invincible, and the thought of provoking such a foe caused a justified sense of dread to consume Lord Veyron.

But at the same time, rage burned amidst his fear. He raged at the knowledge that this masked elf from a foreign land possessed what was undoubtedly his. In Lord Veyron's mind, the sword of Raiken should have passed from leader to leader to mark them as the king's successor. He never understood why the sword was said to have been buried with his ancestor instead of being the symbol of his birthright. But now, he had a chance to fix that. If he could take the sword, and hopefully the breastplate, from his enemy, then he would undoubtedly be crowned king over all humans in Corsallis. Any opposition to his rule would quickly wither in the shadow of his unstoppable power.

All that was left for the would-be king was to take what he felt was rightfully his. The question was how. How could he, without a single piece of the Ascension Armor, wrest the sword away from someone who bore two pieces of the mythical armor? He didn't have a good answer, but that wasn't going to stop him from trying. That sword represented the key to the crown. He'd dreamed of becoming the king since childhood and no obstacle, no matter how great or terrifying, was going to stop him from

obtaining that goal now.

Lord Veyron steadied his horse, lined the steed up, and readied to charge

the thief that stole his ancestor's sword, his inheritance. Despite

witnessing his knight's charge fail so miserably before, Lord Veyron

remained convinced that such an attack was the best offense he could

mount against the legendary armor.

The armored elf saw the look in Lord Veyron's eyes and readied himself

against the predictable charge that the human leader was clearly

preparing. But the armored elf wasn't one to wait around for a challenge

to come to him. Knowing the human's heart, the northern king sprinted

forward, running directly at Lord Veyron and his horse.

Lord Veyron kicked his mount and whipped the reigns. He wanted his

horse to get up to speed quickly. The horse responded as trained, pushing

its hooves sharply into the ground and pushing itself forward with all the

power it could muster with each step. Large clumps of dirt were thrown from the ground and showered down on those fighting nearby as the horse roared past.

The armored elf grinned as he propelled himself foward. He could easily kill the foolish human in a single stroke, but instead, he decided to make an example of Lord Veyron and use his death to his advantage.

#

Riorik's worry about coming up with a plan to discover what was going on between his father's army and the bandits quickly came to an end. The sound of swords clashing and the unmistakable sounds of death rung out from the horde's campsite. Confused, the elf looked at his friends, hoping one of them would know what was going on. Nobody could explain the sounds, but they were all eager to see for themselves.

They wasted no time trying to be sneaky or discreet. The group trampled the bushes and shrubs that hid them with no organization as they rushed back out onto the road. The gnomes swatted limbs and leaves out of their faces as they ran through the foliage while the barbarians trampled most of the greenery in their way. It took significantly less time for the group to

pour out of the hiding spot than it took for them sneak in.

Once outside, the group could clearly see the action unfolding before

them. At first, it looked as though the bandits and the horde were fighting

one another, but Nordahs, thanks to his elven vision, noticed the bandits

on the wall watching the fight.

"It doesn't look like the bandits are fighting. Or at least, not all of them,"

he said to his friends with a curious tone.

It made no sense to the elf that only part of the bandit force would take

up arms against an enemy while the others sat idly by watching. But it was

Rory who cleared their confusion when he spied a familiar symbol among

the flagbearers.

"Those aren't bandits," Rory said. "That's the flag of Tyleco."

"Do you see that one there in the middle?" he asked his friends while

pointing. "That's Lord Veyron, ruler of Tyleco. He's one of the royal line

who fights for the throne."

Ammudien instantly recognized the man that he and Rory had previously

fled from. Riorik had his doubts about the human's visual capabilities

however.

"Are you sure?" the elf asked Rory.

"Yeah, I'm sure. I was Veyron's captain of the guard, remember?" Rory

shot back.

"No need to get hostile," Riorik said, sensing Rory's resentment. "I just

wanted to make sure that you were certain is all."

"Well, what does this mean?" asked Ammudien.

But before anyone could answer, Yafic, who had approached with the

friends were talking, spoke first.

"It means we don't let those human buggers have all the fun," the old

dwarf shouted before running headfirst into the fray.

The dwarves followed in Yafic's footsteps, running to join the fight. This

caused the barbarians, who didn't like to pass up a good brawl, to join in

as well. Even the pint-sized gnomes pushed forward, eager to participate in the fight and exact their revenge on the horde. There was nothing else to discuss for Riorik and his friends as they watched their allies storm the horde's campsite. All they could do was to join in, and join in they did. Riorik unsheathed his sword but not before remembering to slip on the green greaves in his satchel. He would need all the help he could get to even the odds against the horde's leader. He knew his father would be a very tough opponent under any conditions.

"Don't forget this!" Ammudien shouted to Riorik as the gnome pulled Sagrim's shield from the invisible pack, where it had remained safely hidden since the gnome's escape from Tyleco and Lord Veyron.

Riorik was relieved to see the shield. He'd all but forgotten about it in the excitement and chaos. He excitedly grabbed the shield from the gnome, and it instantly resized itself to fit the elf instead of the gnome. The armor's ability to scale itself to match its wearer's size still amazed Riorik, and everyone else for that matter, and the elf was grateful for it at that moment.

Equipped and ready, Riorik moved towards the horde to confront his father again. The young elf realized that at the oasis his father, who had never met his son, didn't recognize him. Cyrel only saw Riorik as competition for the armor, which caused their unnecessary conflict. Or at least that's what Riorik had convinced himself of in the days since. Riorik had completely forgotten that even he didn't know the masked elf's identity until Kirin revealed it.

This time, Riorik was intent on telling his father the truth in an effort to stop the violence and hopefully talk his father into returning home. The greaves and shield were there to protect him long enough to reach his father's position and protect him in case his father's mind was really so gone that there was no hope of recovery.

The elf used the greaves' magic to boost his natural agility and speed. He quickly passed those that had rushed into battle ahead of him. Some of those he passed paused in disbelief at the elf's incredible speed. Even the gnome who knew the greaves were in Riorik's possession was unprepared for just how much the legendary armor elevated Riorik's capabilities. The stories told over the years talked about how the armor could make gods of mortals, but it was never really put into terms that the people hearing those stories could accurately imagine or anticipate.

Riorik came to a stop just short of where Lord Veyron had started his charge. He watched Veyron race toward his target. Part of Riorik wanted to rush to his father's aide but he waited to see how the fight would unfold. Riorik had seen the skills of the masked elf at the oasis, but now he wanted to see how his father would handle a mounted rider at a full gallop. There was little fear in the young elf that Lord Veyron would harm his target, but the Ranger wanted to see what he was capable of. After all, Lord Veyron did attack them too.

#

The horde's elven leader ran towards the charging horse with his shimmering green sword held at an angle from his hip. As the two opponents neared, the elf gripped the sword with both hands, completely covering the weapon's handle, which had been designed to be used with one hand. Lord Veyron, his own sword in hand, held his sword out so that his weapon's hilt was even with his shoulder, ready to strike. Seconds ticked by like hours to the young Ranger as he watched the two prepare to collide, but he couldn't look away.

Lord Veyron eagerly and unwisely leaned forward in his saddle to strike down, but the armored elf made a quick dodge to the side. It looked as if the northern king was trying to dodge the blow, but it was all part of a planned feint.

While Lord Veyron's sword was extended, the self-appointed ruler of Macadre struck. The blade of green ore sliced through the hardened steel of the human's weapon like a knife through butter. Lord Veyron's blade split in two, and the weapon's top half dropped to the ground with a clatter, forcing him to pull back what remained of his sword.

This was a new level of unbelievable power displayed by the stranger. Lord Veyron found the breastplates ability to brush aside even the strongest attacks remarkable before, but now he was in total awe of what his ancestor's sword could do. And seeing his sword cleaved in two so effortlessly by a weapon that remained totally and completely unscathed in the process only increased Veyron's desire to obtain the weapon for himself.

Not to be deterred or so easily dismissed, Lord Veyron pushed himself free of his mount and moved as quickly as he could in his armor to one of his nearby soldiers. Without hesitation or explanation, the human lord took the soldier's unbroken sword right from his hands, replacing it with the broken remains of his weapon.

Armed with a fresh blade, he pointed the sword at his foe and shouted. "Before this day is done, I will have that sword, and you will bow before the one true king!"

"You are no king, but only the puppet of liars and false honor!" the horde's leader shouted back.

The insulting denial of Veyron's presumed authority only angered the human more, exactly as the elf had planned.

Lord Veyron gritted his teeth and squeezed his new sword's handle until his knuckles turned white and his hand ached from the strain. His breathing was heavy, fast, and seething with anger. His emotions had gotten the better of him, causing him to forget his military training and rush forward in a nearly blind rage.

Lord Veyron ran as fast and he could under the weight of his armor, his sword arm outstretched and pointed at the elf, yelling the entire way. The masked elf didn't move. He let his attacker approach, just as he had before during the lance attack. He held his green sword loosely at his side.

Filled with rage, Lord Veyron had apparently forgotten about the power of the breastplate. As he approached, Lord Veyron aimed his blade at the center of the breastplate and thrust as hard as he could. Maybe it was a lapse of judgment to attack the same armor that had deflected his knight's lance at full charge, but all Tyleco soldiers were trained to strike there.

However, unlike before, the elf didn't allow the weapon to strike him this time.

At the absolute last moment, the skilled elven fighter spun on his heels and allowed the blade to pass right by where he'd been. Lord Veyron stumbled forward fully expecting to have his momentum disrupted by the impact. As Lord Veyron stumbled past the elf, the elf made a quick motion from his elbow to rotate his blade's edge around to slice through the charging human's wrist.

The green blade made another effortless and clean slice, severing Veyron's hand. The human's sword fell to the ground with his hand still gripping the handle.

It was the second time in just a few brief minutes that Lord Veyron had been disarmed by his opponent. This time, Lord Veyron lost a little more than just his blade though.

He managed to bring himself to a stop before clutching at the bloody stump where his hand had been just seconds before. The pain and shock prevented him from screaming. He simply stared at the exposed bone and muscle under the river of blood that flooded out from his open arteries. His feelings of anger and rage were replaced with emptiness. The wounded man was emotionally numbed at the sight of his amputated appendage laying motionless on the ground.

The armored elf decided to take advantage of Lord Veyron's catatonic state.

The elf walked up behind the stricken leader of Tyleco and used the improved strength bestowed upon him from the breastplate to deliver a hard, sharp kick to the back of Veyron's knee that sent the wounded man to the ground.

Lord Veyron was forced to catch himself with his remaining hand. The exposed nerves of his open wound throbbed from the contact with the ground and then burned from the dirt that now worked its way inside. In a short period of time, he had gone from being mounted on his horse, looking over the battlefield, and down at his opponent, to being on his hands, or hand and stump, looking up at his enemy. The reality of his situation finally began to sink in for Veyron, and a sense of terror and doom began to well up within him.

The battle between the two was clearly over, but the victor wasn't done with Veyron yet.

"Not much of a king now, are you?" the masked elf taunted the wounded human as he stood over him.

"And what's even funnier is that you actually thought you had the right to call yourself a king. No, I heard the sincerity in your voice. You really think you could be their king," the victorious elf shouted his words to draw the attention of others around him.

The goal was to create disorder among Veyron's troops and supporters. By announcing Veyron's defeat, those loyal to Veyron might be persuaded to abandon the fallen human.

The masked elf bent down, pulled Veyron's helmet away, and pulled his face up to see Darynard. "Do you see that man standing there?" Lord

Veyron said nothing. He was overcome with pain and terror and couldn't speak.

The elf leaned forward, pointing at the bandit king, and spoke directly at Veyron's face. "The real king is there," he told Veyron. "You have no claim to the throne. Only he does. You have been fed lies by your ancestors, who wanted to distort the truth to benefit themselves. They thought that everyone had forgotten the truth. And you humans may have, but I have not. I still remember the truth."

"L-L-Lies," Veyron eventually forced. "I am the one rightful heir. He is but from the line of an illegitimate bastard of a handmaiden."

"Do you hear that Draynard?" the victor called out to the bandit leader, who was still standing at the city's gates. "He says it was your maternal ancestor who was the handmaiden, making you the descendant of the last king's bastard child. I guess it is easier to lie and say someone else was the whore and the bastard when nobody remembers or has the will to speak against those in power."

He turned back to his victim. "But you have it all wrong, Lord Veyron. Oh yes, I know who you are. Would you like to know the truth? I'm afraid you won't care for it though. It is far worse than you may think, but I think now is a good time to educate you on your true lineage."

"It is true, there was a bastard born in the royal family generations ago. And that bastard was born to one of the king's handmaidens. But the bastard child was not the king's child. The handmaiden had secret relations with the king's brother, who tried to claim the child was the king's to place his seed on the throne and deny the rightful heir. The king understandably denied the allegations before exiling his brother, the handmaiden, and their bastard child to live in Tyleco. Embarrassed and ashamed by their exile, the disowned prince along with his commoner wife and their illegitimate son then crafted their story. They decelared they had been sent to Tyleco with a child they claimed to be the king's son and rightful heir to protect him from assassination. That story was passed down from one generation to the next until the truth died with the disgraced prince and his concubine—leaving poor Veyron to know it as the truth instead of the lie it really was."

At this point, the elf's speech had captured Draynard's attention, who'd walked from the city gates towards Lord Veyron and his severed appendage still spilling blood in the dirt.

"So, I am the rightful heir after all?" Draynard asked the masked leader.

"You are, yes. After having exiled his brother, the king fell into a state of depression and sadness, which led him to bouts of heavy drinking and cavorting that probably did not help sway the opinions of those who believed the handmaiden's child was his. But when the queen turned up pregnant, this caused him to straighten up and return to behaving kingly once more. However, his tendencies for gambling, drinking, and such passed to his one and only son. After the king's death, the prince, who was still young at the time, disappeared. He was found in the gambling dens of Brennan before he was taken back to Fielboro and given a coronation that proclaimed him King. Even then, he did not find himself well suited for the throne and would often sneak out of the castle to seek adventure. The new king found his position rather boring and sated his passion for excitement by disguising himself and robbing travelers or running various schemes and gambling rackets in Brennan. This went on for a while before he just disappeared from the castle and never returned. Many assumed he was dead and thus started the fight over the crown. The truth was that he made his home in Brennan, where he felt he belonged more than he did in Fielboro, the true human capital city. The King never took a bride while on the throne but did settle down with someone here, which by rule would make her the queen and their children and their children's descendants the next in line to wear the crown."

"Join me, form the alliance we spoke of and I will make you king. Say no to me and I will conveniently forget the details of your lineage, leaving you to be remembered as the descendant of a handmaiden whore, unworthy to wear the crown."

The horde's leader had drawn a metaphorical line in the sand for Draynard. The time for contemplation was over. The bandit king had to either stand with the unknown individual or stand against him. There was still the threat of a double-cross, but the reminder of his power in the vision of Lord Veyron's severed hand and broken sword were more compelling. If nothing else, having the stranger's support would allow Draynard to live that much longer. The experienced bandit read the writing between the lines, which said that if he refused there was a good chance he would end up bleeding out on the ground just like Veyron.

"You have an alliance," replied Draynard as he waved his hand forward to signal his men to join the fray.

The two sealed the deal with a quick handshake, but the moment was ruined by the wounded Veyron.

"You will never be king. He will betray you. How do you not see it? He has fed you nothing but lies. The moment he no longer needs you he wi—"

Lord Veyron's statement was cut short as Draynard reached down and slit his cousin's throat. Veyron's body went limp. The wounded ruler of Tyleco was finally relieved of the intense, paralyzing pain of the last few moments of life. It wasn't the ending he wanted, but it was an ending he welcomed as he transitioned from life to death.

"I never liked him anyway," the bandit coldly added before dashing off to fight his new ally's fight.

Chapter 9

Riorik could only watch the scene before him in stunned awe. He'd once

listened to his father describe how Draynard was the rightful heir to the

human throne. How was it his father knew the truth but Draynard did not,

Riorik wondered. And then there was the shock of seeing Draynard slit

Veyron's throat. The young elf had seen his fair share of violence and brutality, so death was nothing new to him, but seeing someone kill their own relative in cold blood like that was profoundly disturbing to Riorik.

All the while, Ammudien remained behind Riorik, constantly casting spells to keep the various northern fighters from reaching his dumbstruck friend. The wise gnome knew Riorik needed to see his father's actions and understand the evil in them if the son were to confront the father. The tiny terra mage summoned stone wall after stone wall as he tried to keep Riorik shielded from the attackers' melee weapons and arrows.

For the most part, the horde was focused on Riorik standing near the center of the battlefield with his weapon at his side and his gaze locked on the three leaders before him. Ammudien escaped their notice, free to draw the runes needed for the spells to protect his friend. It worked well at first, but then one dark elf did finally catch a glimpse of the tiny caster after he bounced off one of Ammudien's stone walls, leaving the dark-skinned elf with a bloody broken nose.

The dark elf sought revenge on the magic wielder and immediately hurried in Ammudien's direction.

The gnome mage rushed to ready a defensive spell, but the dark elf moved so quickly that Ammudien wasn't sure he could cast it in time. The gnome's mind raced as he tried to figure out how to defend himself against the rapidly approaching horde fighter, but he drew a blank. The gnome succumbed to fear at that moment, distracted by his concerns for Riorik, who was also defenseless.

Frozen, Ammudien's mind was torn between his own defense and protecting Riorik.

The dark elf raced to within striking distance of the gnome and prepared to thrust his short sword at his small target.

Just as the dark elf swung his blade towards the gnome, a blast of air struck him in the face, blowing the gnome's attacker back and off his feet.

The sight of the dark elf flying backward snapped Ammudien from his temporary daze, and he looked around to find his savior. It was Kirin who'd summoned the powerful gust of wind to protect his diminutive

friend.

But the dark elf would not be so easily defeated. He easily jumped up from

the ground, back onto his feet, and dusted the dirt from his leather garb.

He immediately made a second charge at the gnome.

By this time though, Ammudien had turned his attention back to Riorik's

protection, leaving himself vulnerable again.

Ammudien was willing to ignore the threat of the dark elf and focus on

Riorik because he knew that his elf wizard friend was watching out for

him.

Kirin had not been idle after his wind spell had thrown the dark elf to the

ground. Instead, he'd been busy crafting the runes for his next spell,

confident that another attack would soon follow.

The wizard's new runes were dark, almost black, with a bright green edge.

Kirin flicked his wand through the runes, sending them flying in the

direction of the dark elf. As the runes flew towards their target, they began to coalesce until they formed a sphere. The sphere continued to morph until it transformed into a screaming skull surrounded by the same eerie bright green glow.

When the flying skull and the dark elf intersected, the skull penetrated the elf's cheap leather armor without leaving a mark. It looked as if the magic skull would pass right through the elf, but it never exited through the elf's back. The skull seemed to have been absorbed into the elf's body.

The dark elf's movements came to an immediate halt, and a pained expression came over his face. Kirin could see the dark elf fighting to move as he struggled against the magic's effects, but no amount of fighting could save the dark elf from what happened next.

The dark elf's exposed skin began to bubble as the magic spread throughout his body. Even his face pulsed under the spell's effects. Once the spell had permeated the whole of the dark elf's being, the bubbling of his skin stopped and was replaced by the shriveling of his flesh. His body began to collapse in on itself as the magic rotted the dark elf's insides

away, killing the elf and leaving behind only an empty husk.

Ammudien had watched as the terrifying skull passed directly in front of

him before devouring the dark elf. The gnome was less than thrilled by his

friend's use of forbidden magic, but at the same time, he felt grateful for

Kirin's help.

Between the protective spells he was casting around Riorik, Ammudien did

manage to throw an angry and disapproving look in Kirin's direction. But

Kirin only shrugged at Ammudien's gesture and continued using all the

magic at his disposal to fend off the horde's fighters as well as their new

allies, the bandits.

#

Even with Lord Veyron dead, the knights and soldiers of Tyleco fought on.

The masked elf's plan to scare the soldiers away or lure them to his side

had failed. Many of the human soldiers had simply been too busy fighting

to hear what the horde's leader had to say about their Lord Veyron's heritage. Several hadn't even noticed his corpse sprawled out in a pool of blood.

Veyron's troops had been better equipped than many of the remaining horde fighters. Tyleco had gained the upper hand early in the fight, and a victory was likely for them, though hard fought. Once Riorik and his allies joined the fray, a victory for the defenders of southern Corsallis was all but guaranteed.

But of course, this was before Draynard and the bandits decided to join forces with the horde of invaders.

Their joint forces combined with the defensive positioning and large number of bandits began to tip the scales back into the aggressors' favor to a small degree, but it was still largely an even fight between the two groups. Those bandits fighting outside the city would likely be overcome by the defenders from Mechii eventually, but routing those from inside Brennan could prove a much harder task.

"Riorik!" shouted Ammudien at his stationary friend, snapping the elf from of his trance-like state.

"You need to move. I cannot keep this up forever," the gnome yelled, alluding to his continued and tiring efforts to protect the young elven Ranger.

For the first time in several minutes, Riorik looked around him, seeing the chaos and death that was everywhere. The ground was littered with bodies from both sides. Riorik could see Yafic facing off against a gnoll, the latest of several that had attempted to take on the stout dwarf. Many others had apparently failed, as Yafic stood atop a pile of bodies to better mitigate the attacking gnoll's height advantage.

Despite the apparent skill and fighting capabilities the mound of enemy corpses suggested about Yafic, Riorik made the snap decision to rush to Asbin's father's aid. With the speed of the legendary greaves, Riorik flew to Yafic's position in the blink of an eye. The Ranger did not stop there though. When he reached his new dwarven friend, he swung his blade at the gnoll as he streaked past the beast.

The blow was on target, and the added force from his magically enhanced speed allowed Riorik's blade to slice deep into the gnoll's side, only stopping when steel struck its spine. The jarring sensation of impact at such a high speed sent both Riorik and the gnoll reeling. Riorik was forced to let go of the sword still lodged in the gnoll's spine as he slid to a stop several feet away and tried to stop the shuddering vibrations that reverberated throughout his body.

The gnoll had been knocked down from the force of the impact and lay on the ground, shaking like it was in the throes of seizure.

It took Yafic a second to realize what had happened. He was only able to connect the dots when he saw Riorik's sword protruding from the gnoll's body and Riorik standing just a few feet away. Yafic didn't yet know about Riorik's prized armor, so he couldn't understand how Riorik managed to move so quickly—but he wasn't about to let the opportunity pass him by.

The dwarf had already suffered some wounds in the fight so far, including one serious gash to his cheek and several to his shoulder. The downed gnoll in front of him was a blessing because it meant he could dispose of another beast without endangering himself with their vicious claws.

Armed with a heavy, enormous hammer, Yafic jumped from atop the heap of gnoll corpses and landed near the downed gnoll. He brought down the square-headed hammer down directly on the gnoll's ribs. The sound of cracking ribs, tearing sinew, and squelching organs filled the air. The gnoll let out a single, weak yelp as its last act of life.

Yafic reached down and pulled Riorik's sword from the dead gnoll's body and tossed it to the approaching Ranger.

"Something tells me you're going to need this again, and next time, try to hang onto it," Yafic told Riorik with a wink before moving on to his next target.

The fighting continued to rage on, and the noble defenders were slowly beginning to take control of the battle once again. The bandits had joined against them but not before Riorik's side had inflicted heavy losses on the horde. As confidence in their victory grew, many of the defenders felt a wave of relief coming over them.

But that relief and confidence were short lived.

As the fighting raged on outside the city, Riorik and the others heard a blood-curdling yell, accompanied by the yells of several other unfriendly voices. Those within earshot paused in battle to look for the source of the unexpected sounds. What they saw filled some with dread and others with hope.

It was the horde's remaining forces who'd been left in Kern during the failed ambushes at Mechii and Rhorm. They'd marched west, based on the limited information their sickly informant had gleaned from Lord Veyron. There wasn't much to go on, but somehow, they found their way.

At first, the group had spread out, sweeping vast areas while keeping their course headed westward. Once the fighting had broken out, it was easy to follow sounds of fighting, the thunder of mounted soldiers, and the cries

of death that led them straight to Brennan.

With the arrival of their reinforcements, the tide now favored the

invaders, but the fight was far from over.

#

Riorik noticed the influx of troops in the horde's favor and decided that it

was now or never. He needed to confront his father and reveal their

connection now if there was any hope of convincing him to end the battle.

The Ranger could see the difference in the numbers between the two

forces and knew that the odds were no longer in their favor. If Riorik didn't

act soon, there was a very real chance that Wuffred wouldn't be the only

friend lost in this adventure.

But now the challenge for the elf was to somehow make his way through

the melee to his father's position. The armored king defiantly remained at

the center of the fight, dispatching anyone foolish enough to approach

him from the east. Riorik considered sprinting across the open space between them with his enhanced speed, just as he'd come to Yafic's defense earlier. But he thought better of it. It might be more prudent to use that speed to even the odds between their forces, to give his allies a better chance.

Riorik knew he could use the speed of Ailaire's greaves and the protection of Sagrim's shield to defeat more enemies in a single minute than a dozen of his allies could combined, but the young elf was desperate to speak to his father. It was the whole reason he'd set out on the journey from Rishdel long ago, the mission that had led him here, and he wasn't going to give up on that quest now.

Finally, the conflicted elf decided he would confront his father. He was desperate to understand why his father had left Riorik's family to live in shame all those years ago. To stay and fight might mean that he would never get the answers he so desperately needed to fill that void in his heart.

Choked up by the overwhelming emotions surging through him, Riorik was unable to sprint using the power of his armor. The emotional elf could only manage a walk, his every step filled in equal measure with the hope of reuniting his family and the anger of his father's abandonment.

Riorik moved slowly but with purpose towards the center of the field. His eyes remained locked on where Lord Veyron had been slain and his father still stood. He was filled with a fiery focus. Some of his foes mistook Riorik's slow pace and distant stare as the elf being in a state of shock, thinking he'd make easy pickings.

They were very wrong.

One of the few remaining orcs wobbled towards Riorik with its ungainly gait. Riorik didn't turn his head but watched the orc's approach from the corner of his eye. The orc balled its fist and pulled back to launch a powerful punch at the elf, but before it could complete its strike, Riorik raised Sagrim's shield, swinging it up to collide with the orc's massive fist. The impact between the impenetrable metal shield and the orc's flesh sounded a loud clap. Riorik lowered his shield and continued walking, leaving the orc in a state of disbelief as it looked at the bloody, mangled hand that limply hung from its wrist.

The orc was left vulnerable, surrounded by those eager to take advantage of the opportunity. A knight of Tyleco, one of the few still alive, charged the orc from behind and drove his sword through the orc's thick hide. The beast's sturdy spine deflected the blade, turning it to one side so it missed all the creature's vital organs.

The blow brought the orc back from its stunned state, and it began thrashing about in pain. The knight struggled to hold onto his blade's grip, fearing that the orc's flailing would wrest the blade free of the wound, releasing the orc to turn on its attacker.

But as luck would have it, the knight's grasp and the beast's thrashing together caused the blade to thrust deeper into the wound, opening the gash wider. Now, even if the orc managed to remove the sword, it was bleeding so profusely that it would certainly die.

But the knight did not stop there. Encouraged by the growing size of the wound and the increasing fervor in which the orc struggled, the knight attempted to work the blade in the opposite direction to the orc's movements. The wound grew, and eventually, the knight violently ripped his sword through orc's weakened hide. The blade left a massive hole in the beast's side and managed to pull a waterfall of intestines out with it. Eviscerated, the orc's movements slowed before it completely succumbed to blood loss. It crashed to the ground, much to the knight's delight.

Meanwhile, Riorik continued his slow march toward his father, and still others tried to attack him. A gnoll approached, seeming to ignore what Riorik had so casually done to the orc. The gnoll dropped to all fours and sprinted towards Riorik, using its lower profile and faster speed to gain the advantage over the elf.

Just as the gnoll neared Riorik, the hairy beast jumped into the air with its mouth open and claws out, ready to bite and slash its poor victim.

But Riorik had no intention of being the gnoll's victim.

For the first time since he decided to confront his father, the elf managed to call upon the power of the greaves to take a running jump towards the flying gnoll. The elf raised his knee with its green armor covering as he leaped at the gnoll. The two clashed in mid-air, with Riorik's knee meeting the unsuspecting and unprepared gnoll's jaw. The impenetrable armor combined with the speed of the jump allowed the elf's knee to shatter the gnoll's jawbone to bits, sending gnoll's teeth raining to the ground.

The gnoll stumbled back under the force of the blow, its back hitting the ground just feet from where it had leapt. Riorik landed next to the dazed gnoll, and before it could regain its senses, Riorik's sword pierced through the gnoll's fur, directly into its heart. The gnoll's life faded away quickly and quietly. Riorik withdrew his sword from the body and continued walking forward.

For the most part, those who'd seen what the elf had done to the gnoll and the orc didn't dare try their luck against him themselves. But there were a bold few who thought they stood a better chance—they did not.

Some Riorik was forced to fight, briefly, before killing, but others were deflected easily, only to be set upon by the elf's allies. Either way, Riorik's approach to the center of the battlefield was unhindered.

In a few moments, Riorik reached his destination. The young Ranger stared at the horde's leader, who stared back at Riorik. The standoff between the two was tense for a few seconds before either elf moved or spoke.

Chapter 10

"You're as foolish as you are young," chuckled the horde's leader as Riorik approached.

"I'm not a fool. I have been seeking you all this time," replied Riorik.

Riorik's words caught the elf by surprise. Then, the invading elf remembered Ammudien calling out to him with the name Cyrel.

"So, you seek Cyrel Leafwalker do you?" the masked elf asked, the name crossing his lips for the first time in many years.

"I do," answered Riorik plainly.

"And who is Cyrel Leafwalker to you? You're too young to know that name," the confused invader added.

"Have you forgotten your own face?" Riorik asked. "Or have you been hidden behind that mask for so many years that you've forgotten what you look like?"

The masked elf did not understand Riorik's meaning.

"I am fully aware of my own appearance. What would knowing my own face have to do with you?" the invader asked.

"Because this is your face," Riorik said pointing at his own face. "Mother always said that I looked just like you."

"Ahh, I see now," the masked elf replied, connecting the dots.

"I didn't know your mother was with child when I left," he added.

"Well, she was. And your disappearance left her to raise me alone in the shadow of the shame you left behind," Riorik said angrily. He embraced the resentment he'd harbored for so long against his father for making his mother live in such misery.

"And now what? You want me to stop what I'm doing, return home, and all will be forgotten. Is that it? Is that why you sought me out?"

Hearing the words aloud, it all sounded a bit silly and childish to Riorik. But still, the elf remained devoted to his cause, even if it meant his father was returned to Rishdel as a prisoner. At least then perhaps Riorik and his mother could get some answers. At least then the village's discontent could be aimed at Cyrel and not Bjiki.

Riorik's love for his mother spurred him on, even if it meant accepting that the loving father he'd hoped for was now corrupt and evil. The goal was to remove the shame from his family, but Riorik felt content with the idea of just being able to take that shame away from his doting mother.

"All may not be forgotten, but it's time for you to return home. This invasion of yours is folly. The gnomes rejected you. The dwarves rejected you. And now they fight together alongside the barbarians—against you. All you've managed to do is tear down the walls that have divided the people of this land for so long, united them against a common enemy. You. You will not find victory here, nor will you be able to restore the honor lost by your own actions. All that's left for you is to be the Ranger everyone said you were and take responsibility for your actions, both old and new."

Riorik's plea did little to sway the mind of his father.

"There will be no authority but mine by the time I'm done. If you seek a family reunion, then stand beside me or else the Leafwalker family will suffer another loss."

It was not really the invitation Riorik wanted.

"The Leafwalker family has lived in shame long enough because of your actions. I will not invite more shame upon our name by making the same mistakes as you. I will stay on the side of right and honor."

Riorik knew that declining the offer would likely anger his father, but he also knew he wouldn't find honor or joy in a reunion supported by ruthless violence and dishonorable acts.

"I'd rather return to Rishdel fatherless but honorable, to lift the burden you left for my mother to carry in your absence rather than follow in your shameful ways. That would only add to her already insurmountable load."

"Ah, the shortsightedness of the young," the other elf mused. "If you join me and we are victorious in our conquest over those who would deny us our true power, the Leafwalker name would be feared, not shunned. The Leafwalker family would consist of elves of great importance. No shame could cling to any family in such a prosperous and powerful position. If you truly want to remove the stain of shame from the name Leafwalker, remove those who imposed that shame upon you and your mother. You and I both know that it was not my actions but the judgment of the council that cast you and your mother under that suffocating shadow. But together, we can remove the council."

It filled Riorik with sadness to hear the defiance and hatred in the words of his father. Riorik knew that he'd have no choice to but fight if he was to find honor. As much as he hated it, he was beginning to feel that the only way his father return to Rishdel would be as a corpse.

No son ever dreams of killing their father, but Riorik felt he had no choice. He wore the remaining Ascension Armor. He was the only one on the battlefield who stood a chance against someone wearing the other pieces. The young Ranger readied himself against the veteran Ranger. Riorik set his feet, pushing them into the ground and grinding out small depressions he could use for leverage to push off from when the time came. He raised Sagrim's shield in front of him while holding his sword next to it, ready to counter his foe.

The elder elf entered a combat stance himself, but without the aid of the legendary shield.

They stared at each other, waiting to see who would strike first.

Considering his father's sword was far superior and he wore a breastplate that Riorik's sword couldn't pierce, Riorik was hesitant to attack.

Likewise, the armored elf still remembered the explosive interaction between the shield and the sword at the oasis, and he wasn't excited at the prospect of repeating that event again as his trusty wizard had never returned with an explanation.

"Nice helmet," Riorik eventually said, trying to taunt his opponent into action by referring to the still crumpled helmet. "Shame it wasn't as robust as the rest of your armor, it might have spared you that nice scar."

"Yes, a shame," the other elf said as he reached up and massaged the still tender wound on his brow from where the helmet had been caved in. "I suppose the same could be said for your friend though too. It might have spared him from death. But probably not."

The two continued to taunt each other as they started circling, eyes locked and bodies ready to pounce. Neither elf was taking the bait though. Riorik accused his father of being ineffective in his hunt for the armor because Riorik and his friends found two pieces in a short period of time. Meanwhile, his father pointed out how poorly Riorik used the equipment, failing to stop the slaughter of hundreds, if not thousands of people. The insults and accusations went on and on but neither flinched.

Eventually, Riorik ran out of patience.

"You're coming home with me one way or another, Father!" Riorik yelled before charging his opponent.

In anger, Riorik foolishly charged his father with the magical shield held firmly in front of him. He never got close to his mark though. As Riorik charged forward, the more seasoned elf waited until he got near, then kicked up dirt in Riorik's face. Riorik instinctively raised his shield in response, covering his face and losing sight of his target. The veteran Ranger seized the opportunity and deftly spun out of Riorik's path. When

Riorik lowered the shield and realized his mistake, the young elf quickly spun around in panic, thinking he was about to be stabbed in the back. Fortunately for Riorik, no such attack came. Instead, the taunting resumed.

"You wear the greaves of our ancestors but fail to use them when they could benefit you most. Pathetic," the elf taunted Riorik.

Riorik ran forward again, this time using the speed and agility of the greaves to launch a lightning-quick attack.

His father expected just such an attack in response to his taunt. The older elf had lowered his sword in anticipation of Riorik's blitz and stood with his free hand toward his attacker. As Riorik approached at an unnatural speed, the young elf's target raised his free hand with his palm facing out and pushed forward through the air as hard as he could.

The elf's unexpected counterattack was timed perfectly.

Riorik ran forward, blinded by his anger and youth. He held his shield extended in front of him, creating a large surface for his father to strike at.

The older elf's forceful palm thrust landed against the shield as Riorik's arm had reached maximum extension. The power of the thrust brought Riorik to a jarring standstill as his arm gave way and he crashed into the shield now against his opponent's palm.

Wanting to take advantage of Riorik's stunned state, the older elf tried to quickly land a stab. Fortunately for Riorik, he was able to recover in time and move his shield to block the blow. The magic in the two pieces of equipment repelled one another, preventing the sword from doing any damage.

This angered Riorik's father, who still didn't understand the cause of the interactions between the legendary armor pieces.

Enraged by his recent failure to at least wound Riorik, he now went on the offensive.

At first, he bull rushed Riorik, hoping that with enough determination, the power of the breastplate and sharpness of the sword would do as he willed, do what they had just failed to do, what they failed to do at the oasis. However, Riorik was eager to avoid another explosive encounter, so the young elf used the agility granted by his greaves to dodge the uncharacteristically clumsy attack from the older, more experienced fighter.

Riorik knew that his sword had no chance of penetrating the breastplate and couldn't withstand any contact with the green sword's blade. He was forced to bide his time until he could manage a strike at either the legs or the head. And seeing how this was his father, Riorik didn't want to take the chance of killing his him with a blow to the head. He would wait for the perfect opening to attack the legs, and the legs only. He might not get an opportunity however, since his father often stood with his sword lowered to protect the weak spot in his equipment, and for Riorik to drop low enough to manage such an attack would mean that he would be forfeiting not only the speed of the greaves but also their protection.

It was a tricky situation for the young elf to be in, but as the two squared

off against one another, Riorik felt confident that he could return to

Rishdel with his father this day.

They took turns launching attacks at each other. Riorik used his speed and

the shield to dodge and repel his father's attacks while trying to create an

opening to attack his legs. Meanwhile, the more experienced fighter, who

was still flustered by his failure to land any attacks on Riorik, resorted to

using every trick at his disposal to disorient him.

Dirt and dust flew as the two moved about, and some because it was

thrown in Riorik's face from time to time, but neither elf could gain the

advantage over the other, or land a single blow. The battle raged on

around them, but the elves were only aware of the fight in front of them.

They performed exactly as both Rangers had been trained back in Rishdel.

#

The arrival of the remaining forces from Kern had been a saving grace for

the invaders and their new bandit allies. The remaining archers in Kern quickly zeroed in on the archers from Tyleco, raining down arrows on the fallen lord's ranged troops. The unsuspecting archers from Tyleco didn't stand a chance against the dark, heavy, cast iron-tipped arrows that showered them. The invaders had equipped their arrows to ensure maximum armor penetration. Even if the rather brittle arrowheads broke on impact, the sheer force of the weighty projectiles was still enough to wound or disorient any soldier, and their compromised armor would succumb to the next arrow.

It took only a few quick volleys for the invaders to all but eliminate Lord Veyron's archers, who had been instrumental in the battle up until this point, giving the defending people of Corsallis a fair chance at victory over the invaders. With the archers gone, the fighting would be more intense for those in close combat, but the fighting was already so frantic that nobody noticed the archers stopped firing.

Only after Tyleco's archers had been defeated did the invader's archers take notice of the seemingly undefended gnomes lined up casting spell after spell. The tiny gnomes had escaped their eyes at first. The invader's archers had instinctively attacked the source of the enemy's volleys so they could take out that threat first and in doing so, completely overlooked the line of mages practically standing directly in front of them. Now that the archers had seen the gnomes, they instantly recognized the threat to their colleagues and shifted targets. However, the mages were not as defenseless as they had at first appeared. The first volley of arrows from the invaders all smacked against an invisible wall protecting the mages. The sounds of dozens of arrows slamming into their protective spell caught the attention of several mages.

It was now an archer versus mage showdown as several of the mages turned to take on the archers. However, the magic that protected the gnomes from the archers also protected the archers from the gnomes. The mages had to either take down the magical barrier that shielded them from the arrows, or the mages had to move outside of the protective spell's cover. They couldn't cast spells through it. The spell was great for protecting and defending the mages, but it also created an obstacle for them too in this case.

The first gnomes to step out from the defensive spell worked to distract the archers with magical flashes of light, small fire spells that could ignite the grass or cloth armor worn by the archers, and even stone rain that pelted the archers with small rocks. As the gnomes barraged the archers with these minor spells, other mages began to use the opportunity to summon more devastating spells that required more time to create. Soon other spells like fireballs began to inflict moderate damage against the archers and their flammable equipment, and bolts of lightning struck multiple archers at a time. But it was the wind mages that had the biggest effect. Three wind mages summoned whirlwind spells at different ranges between them and the archers. Two whirlwinds raged in the space between the gnomes and the archers, snagging any arrows flying in the gnomes' direction and blowing the archers off balance. The final whirlwind was cast at the archers' rear and scattered the archers with its strong gusts of wind, separating many of the archers from their bows while littering the ground with the dozens and dozens of arrows that had been safely carried in the archers' quivers.

Content that the archer threat had been nullified, or at least seriously diminished, the mages returned to their positions on the other side of the shield spell and resumed their work.

During the duel, the invading archers had only managed to strike down two of the mages before they were overcome by the whirlwinds. The archers that remained slowly collected themselves and what few viable bows and arrows they could find strewn across the ground. Equipped again, the archers fled into the nearby bushes, eager to find a better position to rain down revenge on the tiny mages.

#

Riorik and his father continued to attack each other back and forth, but still neither had the advantage. Riorik's speed made him a difficult target to hit while his father's superior strength kept the younger elf at a distance. There were times where the two got close, but the repelling power of their armor forced them apart, preventing them from inflicting serious damage on each other. And despite the increased power from the breastplate and agility from the greaves, both elves were beginning to grow tired and slow down.

It was shaping up to be a stalemate.

However, among the chaos, Riorik failed to notice Draynard's approach. The bandit stood by and watched the last several failed attacks while assessing the situation. Draynard was in awe of Riorik's impressive speed, but he was simultaneously wowed by his new ally's show of unbridled strength. A strength that was far superior to anything or anyone else on the battlefield.

But finally, as Draynard stood watching, Riorik managed to land a blow against his father that looked to be a game changer.

The young elf had been using his greaves to accelerate forward, throwing feints to trick his father into attacking so that he could counter, but his father never gave in to Riorik's attempts. Finally, Riorik changed tactics

and charged to his target's side, sprinting past the defending elf. Riorik

swung his sword's edge behind him as he flew past his father's position.

The blade sliced the back Cyrel's calf, which erupted in pain as he hobbled,

fighting to stay upright while blood trickled down the back of his leg.

Riorik sensed the opportunity to end the fight and disarm his father.

"If I can get that sword away from him, then he'll have no choice but to

surrender. Then we can return to Rishdel and hope the elders can find a

way to clear the corruption that has obviously clouded his mind," the

young elf thought to himself as he prepared to deliver a fight-ending blow.

Riorik steadied the shield of Sagrim and prepared to call upon the greaves

one more time. He looked at his father's face, but instead of seeing fear or

defeat, Riorik saw glee. His father was smiling at him. It was an eerie smile

that filled Riorik with dread in his moment of victory. It was most

unnerving to the young Ranger, just as his father's efforts to walk towards

Riorik were.

Just as Riorik pushed off with his feet, his attack was interrupted. Metal clanged against the elf's shield as a hook caught the shield's edge. Riorik felt a strong tug that forced him to abandon his attack to secure the shield. Without the shield, he was too exposed against his father. It was imperative that Riorik retained the shield.

Riorik spun in the direction of the hook's pull. He looked straight at Draynard. The bandit had skillfully tossed a grappling hook to snare the shield and was now working to dislodge the legendary item from Riorik's grip. The unexpected diversion panicked the young elf, whose only thought was to hold onto the shield. Riorik completely forgot about his approaching father and the speedy greaves that still covered his legs. He dropped his sword and grabbed the shield with both hands as he fought against the bandit's pull.

Riorik was distraught and totally oblivious to the threat that was now standing beside him.

The older elf took his shiny green sword and effortlessly thrust it through Riorik's side, slicing between the young elf's ribs. It cut through the elf's lungs, piercing his ribcage on the other side.

The cut was so clean with the blade's sharp edge that it took a moment for Riorik to feel any pain. Riorik's eyes opened wide at the realization of what had just happened to him. He began to repeatedly blink his eyes in a silent state of shock, but that soon passed as the pain began to radiate throughout his body. He turned to his attacker and saw his father, who was standing directly next to Riorik, eye to eye.

"I'm not who you think I am. Cyrel Leafwalker has been dead for years," the elf whispered in Riorik's ear.

"You can drop the lie," Riorik gasped as he strained to regain consciousness. "Mother told me about what happened. How you killed Shadrack in the forest."

His father let out a loud laugh.

With Riorik firmly impaled on the sword, his father used his other hand to throw his helmet clear of his head, giving Riorik an unobstructed view of his face for the first time.

Riorik looked, but he didn't see his face as expected. His mother had told him for years that Riorik strongly resembled his father, Cyrel. But the face Riorik saw didn't resemble his own. While elves shared a lot of physical features, Riorik could see enough differences to know that this elf didn't look like him.

Riorik's attacker could see the confusion in Riorik's eyes.

"Don't you see it?" he asked Riorik. "I'm not Cyrel. I *am* Shadrack!"

A sense of clarity washed over the fading Riorik. In that moment, he understood that his father had never betrayed the Rangers or his friend, but it was his friend who had betrayed him. Riorik and his family had lived in shame when his father had instead been murdered by the elf he trusted most. And now, it seemed that Riorik would meet the same fate.

Knowing that he was out of time, Riorik did the only thing he could with the last of the life left in him.

"NORDAHS!" he yelled as loud as he could while using what energy was left in his legs to push himself towards the bandit still tugging on the shield.

The effort forced Shadrack Bladeleaf to pull his sword from Riorik's body or else see the magical blade swept away with Riorik's movement. This left Riorik free to blast towards Draynard.

The elf flew towards the unprepared Draynard, shield first. The shield slammed into Draynard's face with the force of Riorik's charge, shattering his under and sending him to the ground unconscious.

Riorik landed on top of the bandit and gasped as his body struggled to draw breath despite his mortal wound.

Nordahs rushed to his friend's side and desperately tried to think of some way to save his friend's life.

"It's your father, not mine," Riorik whispered with his final breath.

Nordahs could only watch as Riorik lost consciousness and died. Riorik's final words didn't make sense to the young elf at first. As tears began to roll down his cheeks, his soul was filled with anger and rage at the loss of his best friend. Nordahs raised his head, and through his teary eyes, he looked upon the face of his friend's murderer. It was then that Riorik's words made sense.

Nordahs couldn't remember his father, but his mother had a painting commissioned of her and Shadrack before Nordahs' birth, which hung in their home. He'd looked at that painting thousands of times, to the point that he could picture his father's likeness in his mind. The elf he saw out there on the battlefield, clad in the shimmering green breastplate and holding the green blade covered in his friend's blood, wore the face from his mother's painting.

The invader wasn't Riorik's father, but his own. His father hadn't died in the forest all those years ago, but instead, he plotted to overthrow the leaders of Corsallis in a bloodthirsty attempt to take it all for himself. But

Nordahs couldn't understand how his father had survived. If the elves found a body they thought was his, but he was here now, who was the decapitated elf in the woods, and how did Shadrack find the sword? These were questions Nordahs couldn't answer, but he knew who could— his father.

Nordahs gently laid his friend's corpse back to the ground before taking his kukri's in hand and marching straight towards his father.

"How could you? You killed my friend! For what? Why did you leave Mother and I? Why did you make us think you were dead for all these years? What the hell have you done?" Nordahs screamed as he marched toward Shadrack. "Explain yourself! Now!"

Chapter 11

The force of Riorik's cry and Nordahs' furious demands captured Kirin's attention. In a second, the elf wizard took in his brother's body on the ground and Nordahs striding angrily towards Kirin's former master.

Kirin was stunned to see the armored elf had removed his helmet. For the first time, Riorik's brother looked upon the face of the elf who'd convinced Kirin he was his father.

Even at a distance, Kirin could tell he didn't resemble the father he remembered, nor did he resemble Riorik. The older elf was clearly not their father. Kirin was filled with anger at the deception and curious to know just who had tricked him.

When Cyrel and Shadrack had disappeared, Kirin was still young. His memories were few, mostly fuzzy images and the faint sounds of their voices. But Kirin soon realized that the deception was his own doing. The other elf had never truly claimed to be his father, but rather Kirin assumed he was because of his familiar voice. Kirin had taken it for granted that the familiar voice belonged to his father since he believed Shadrack was dead. The realization that Kirin's own wrong assumption had also misled Riorik left the elven wizard with a crushing sense of responsibility for his brother's death. Kirin was filled with self-loathing, anger, and a deep regret. Not only was Kirin overwhelmed by Riorik's death, but he also knew he would soon face the painful task of having to tell their mother about her child's demise. Worst of all, his guilt in the matter would need to be confessed.

"Nordahs, what happened? Is Rio dead? Is my brother dead?" Kirin shouted at Nordahs as he came closer to Riorik's body.

Nordahs was too focused on Shadrack to heed Kirin's questions. Instead, Nordahs stormed toward his father.

"Tell me what happened right now!" Nordahs demanded. "Explain why you left me and Mother to think you were dead! Tell me what happened to Cyrel. Tell me this instant!"

Shadrack watched Nordahs drawing nearer and simply grinned again.

"Ahh, so you're the spawn of my wife's womb. I'm glad it's you and not that idealistic, feeble excuse for an elf," Shadrack replied.

Shadrack's words incensed both Nordahs and Kirin further. Neither could stand the insult to their noble, kind-hearted friend and brother, especially when he lay lifeless, mere feet away.

"I can see my spirit burning within you. Your friend seemed only full of hope and an unfortunate sense of honor, just like his father. It was those same traits that killed his father too."

Again, Shadrack's comments only fanned the flames of anger in Kirin and Nordahs.

"Just tell me what you did!" Nordahs screamed at his father.

"Are you sure you really want to know?" Shadrack asked his son, who came to a halt just a few feet from his father.

Nordahs managed a slight jerk of his head in response to his father's question. The young elf was slowly returning from that initial state of rage. He was beginning to comprehend the reality of the situation—not just that his father was the one who'd led this invasion, but also how much peril Nordahs himself was in, being so close to someone who was obviously very dangerous.

"Are you crazy? Did you really just think you could walk up and do anything to him? Look at what happened to Riorik and he was wearing the armor. You have nothing! He will massacre you," Nordahs began to think

to himself about his current predicament. His concern was growing.

Meanwhile, Shadrack had turned his attention to Kirin, who'd also moved

a little closer into danger. He too was anxious to understand how Shadrack

was there and not his father, Cyrel.

"Traitor!" Shadrack yelled at Kirin.

Shadrack hadn't failed to miss Kirin's participation in the fight on the side

of the defenders. All things considered, Shadrack wasn't terribly surprised,

but he was still irritated at Kirin's betrayal. However, Shadrack failed to

see his own actions in making Kirin think he was the young wizard's father

as a betrayal of Kirin's trust. The older elf was so consumed with his own

mission that he completely failed to see the irony.

Disregarding Kirin's duplicity, Shadrack opted to use the situation to his

advantage rather than launch an immediate attack.

"If you and Kirin would like to know the truth, I will require Kirin cast a spell to offer us a bit of protection. The answer you want will take time, and I have no interest in your pesky little friends interrupting me."

Kirin was just as curious as Nordahs to understand the truth now that everything they'd believed for several years had been revealed to be untrue. If Shadrack was willing to tell them what happened in exchange for a spell, Kirin was more than willing to oblige.

The elven wizard set about drawing a rune on the ground, dragging his wand through the dirt and making a line that connected to the next rune. He continued the pattern until the ring of runes encircled the three elves. With the final rune drawn and connected, Kirin pushed the tip of his wand into the glowing line that joined all the runes and then flicked his wand up into the air, sending the runes flying.

A translucent wave rippled through the air like a see-through curtain, rising from the ground to surround the elves. The wave reached about a foot over their heads and created a seamless dome over them. It was a barrier spell, like the magic that had protected Mechii during Shadrack's siege, but much less powerful.

Kirin's barrier could stop several arrows and a few melee attackers, but not for long. The power of the ancient magic was lost, so this was the best the elven wizard could manage, and he hoped it would be enough to hear Shadrack's tale.

"Done. Now talk fast, it may not last long," Kirin told Shadrack as the spell finished taking shape.

Shadrack started by addressing Kirin.

"You've grown much since the last time you laid eyes on your father. I noticed when we first met at the oasis."

Kirin wasn't interested in his own growth though.

"Yeah, I've grown. It's what we do over the years, so it's kind of expected. But we're not here to talk about my height. We're here, like this, now, so that you can tell us what you've done and why my brother had to die," Kirin responded bitterly, his teeth clenched.

"My, my, aren't we testy," Shadrack shot back, sensing Kirin's anger.

Nordahs interrupted before the animosity between the two derailed the

conversation. He needed answers to the questions that brought them to

this point.

"The protection you wanted has been given. Just tell us what you've done.

Why are we here talking to you and not Cyrel?" Nordahs interjected,

hoping to return the discussion to what was important.

Shadrack snapped back towards Nordahs and gave him the same wry grin

that had stretched across his face through much of the interaction. The

father then approached his son.

Nordahs cautiously took a step back as Shadrack neared. His grin was

replaced by a scowl as Shadrack stopped once more.

"Hmph," Shadrack huffed, "a coward just like the other one."

"Just tell me what I want to know," Nordahs sternly shot back.

"Impatient, I see," Shadrack replied to his son. "Just like your father. Very

well, I will tell you what you want to know, but first, you both must lay down your arms. If you want a monologue, I will give you one, but I will not be attacked while telling you what you want to know."

There was much hesitation between Nordahs and Kirin, but eventually, the Ranger laid his curved daggers on the ground and the wizard calmly placed his wand in the dirt at his feet.

Both of them understood the relative futility of fighting Shadrack at this point. Nordahs would be overpowered by his father's superior equipment, while Kirin's magic would pose as much of a threat to himself and Nordahs as it would to Shadrack while they were confined within the protective barrier. The young wizard wasn't foolish enough to risk a spell rebounding or reflecting off the barrier and hitting him or his friend. Ultimately, they both decided to comply, as it seemed the least risky option, at least for the time being.

Satisfied and rather surprised by the compliance of the two young elves, Shadrack settled in to tell his tale.

"It is true, Cyrel and I were among the top Rangers in the guild. Cyrel ranked above me, so I acted as his second in command, but truth be told, Cyrel wasn't the Ranger everyone believed him to be. He was noble and honorable, devoted to the guild and its mission, but he was far from the master tactician and skilled fighter his reputation claimed him to be. He stood out among the recruits, but in the real world, Cyrel was indecisive and often incapable of doing what needed to be done."

Shadrack paused at this point and looked directly at Kirin.

"That is, if he wasn't ordered to do so, he lacked the courage to kill when it was needed. He lacked the fortitude to take that final step."

Shadrack then turned to look at Nordahs.

"That wasn't a shortcoming I shared with Cyrel. When killing was needed and he could not deliver, I did. Without qualm or hesitation, I would kill when he could not—when the need arose."

At this point, Shadrack stood silent, seeming lost in reflection on the days he spent as a Ranger standing beside Cyrel. The hardness in his face grew as he recalled those times. They apparently weren't happy memories for

Shadrack.

"It is true, Cyrel and I were friends in the beginning. But, as time wore on,

that friendship eroded until all that was left were the responsibilities and

courtesies demanded by our ranks. He took credit for my efforts and

received accolades and titles that should've been mine. My willingness to

do what he couldn't allowed us to return to Rishdel and claim numerous

victories I was never recognized for.

"At first, I naively assumed that given his higher rank that he would be

recognized first and my recognition would come next. But that recognition

never came. Not from the elders, and certainly not from Cyrel. He grew

accustomed to being showered with adoration, with the rewards earned

from my sweat and my blade. Never once did he give me credit for

anything in his mission reports to the elders. He was content to keep that

honor for himself. Only later did I discover that he'd intentionally advised

the elders against promoting me to an equal rank or giving me my own troops to command. He never admitted it, even when I confronted him on the subject, but I knew he'd done so. He knew that if I was given my own command, then his ineffectiveness would be revealed and I would get the respect and honors that he'd come to covet only for himself.

"Then, after that last fight in the forest, when he returned to Rishdel addle-minded, I thought my time had finally come. I expected the elders to promote me to Cyrel's position while he remained at home in that befuddled state. But I was wrong. The elders ordered the entire troop to take time to rest and visit their families. I was forced to sit by and watch while the elders waited for their hero's mind to return, so confident in his abilities that they preferred to forego his troop's protection rather than see them under the command of another. To their minds, there was no one else who could lead those elves with the success of the great Cyrel Leafwalker. When I approached the elders to suggest I take the others on a few scouting missions, just to keep their skills sharp, the elders refused to let anyone other than Cyrel lead them.

"Even in his stupefied and worthless state, Cyrel stood in my way. He prevented me from showing the elders my true potential, my true worth.

"So, I went to his house to speak with him. I wanted to see for myself just how bad his condition was. I hoped I could determine how much longer I'd be forced to sit in the shadows, my skills going to waste while the elders clung to their false perceptions of their great Ranger. He spoke to me about finding something in the woods and needing to return there, and I thought this might be my opportunity to rid myself of Cyrel once and for all.

"I agreed to escort Cyrel into the woods, since that was all his muddled mind could focus on. The plan was to keep him there until we ran across some beast that meant us harm so I could leave the dazed Cyrel to his doom. With their great hero dead, the elders would have little choice but to replace him, and being his second in command, I would naturally be the obvious choice. But things did not go as planned.

"The two of us had gotten only a few hundred yards into the forest when I could start to see a change in Cyrel's condition. There was a strength to his voice that had been absent since our return. His speech evolved from half-finished thoughts and stutters into more descriptive, animated terms, a sign that his mental acuity was returning. We followed the river near the forest's eastern edge and climbed steep a hill. There, he led me straight to a hole at the top the hill, and things really began to change.

"He walked directly into the hole, dropping through the opening and inside the hill itself. Stunned and curious, I followed him. Once I landed on the stone floor beneath the opening, I realized the hill hid a tomb, but I was still unaware of whose tomb it was and what it contained. What I did know, however, was that Cyrel's mind had completely returned. He looked at me with clear eyes for the first time since our return to Rishdel. He smiled at me as though he noticed I was there for the first time that day.

"'Shadrack, it's here!' he said. 'The sword of Raiken is here. The stories are true!' He was absolutely convinced of it, I could hear it in his voice. I tried to reason with him, to tell him those stories were just that—stories, but he was adamant that not only was it real but that it was there, in that tomb. Since my words weren't getting through to him, I decided to play along and asked him to show me. He walked right over to the stone sarcophagus where Lord Raiken's body was laid to rest and pulled the glowing blade from the stone sheath engraved into the stone coffin's surface. He held it out for me to see. As much as I didn't want to believe it, there was no denying the sword's existence and the effect it seemed to have on Cyrel. Just holding the blade in his hands made him seem more mentally capable than he had before, but more than that, he seemed to exude a confidence that I hadn't seen in him for some while.

"Regardless, once he had found the blade—the object that seemingly beckoned him back to the tomb—he was ready to return to Rishdel. And so, we pulled ourselves from the tomb and began walking back to the village. I knew that with his return, my chance to lead would be gone. I tried to reason with him that we should keep the sword and use it for ourselves. But his sense of honor and devotion was at its greatest then. He refused, saying that it was our obligation to turn over the sword to the elders and that it would be their obligation to return it to the rightful heir of the humans. I mean, here was a sword of unrivaled power and Cyrel wanted to give it away out of his pathetic sense of honor. He believed that for either of us to hide the sword's existence would be theft and fraud, 'two things unbecoming of a Ranger of Rishdel.'

"It was then that I realized that if the sword were returned to Rishdel, then Cyrel would continue to play the hero and I would forever be condemned to live in his shadow, denied my true potential. And so I confronted him about my being rejected for promotion, to which he replied, 'But I need you to stay where you are.' It was confirmed for me then that he wasn't my friend but an abuser of my talents and a thief of the honors I had earned. He chastised me that theft and fraud were ugly traits for a Ranger, even though he'd done it for years and obviously intended to continue. He had some nerve to lecture me about something he was more guilty of than me.

"I decided I wouldn't continue to be the fool whose shoulders Cyrel stood upon any longer. I decided I would take the sword from Cyrel and use it to claim what was rightfully mine. He would have no choice but to go along with the plan if I held the sword—or so I thought. The only problem was that he clung to the blade like a new parent to their child. There was no way to take the sword from Cyrel without a fight, a fight the sword would give him the advantage in.

"Instead, I pulled the sword that hung in a sheath from his hips. He spun to face me with a look of surprise in his eyes. He fumbled with the sword in his hands, I presume to use it in his defense, but I didn't give him time to try. I thrust his own sword deep into his chest, drove him to the ground and took his prize as my own.

"In that instant, I knew two things to be absolutely certain. One, that if I returned to Rishdel without Cyrel, there would be loads of questions from the elders that I wouldn't be able to answer and would undoubtedly result in a search for his body. And two, that even if I did return with the sword, the elders would surely take it away from me and deny me once again. I concluded that if I were to ever have the honors I was owed, I would have to take them as nobody seemed willing to give them when due.

"In life, Cyrel had been content to use my efforts to further his own cause, and in death, Cyrel would loom over my existence, casting doubt as to my involvement in his death or raising questions about my ability to lead if I'd left my befuddled commander to die in the forest. The more I thought about it, the more I came to realize that my life among the Rangers was over. A life of exile was all that was left for me, but I refused to be on the run in that exile.

"Over the years, others had often remarked how similar Cyrel and I looked, often assuming we were brothers or suggesting that we shared a father. After several minutes of contemplation alone in the woods, I decided I would use this as my source of escape.

"I swapped clothes with Cyrel's body, careful to slide his sword back through the same wound to avoid any evidence that might expose my ruse. Then, wearing Cyrel's bloodied tunic and with his corpse dressed in mine, I took Raiken's sword and chopped off Cyrel's head, the only physical feature that would obviously give my plan away. I stuffed his head into my rucksack and headed north into exile, where I vowed to assemble my own forces before returning and taking from the elders what they had so long denied me—proper respect.

"Being an elf and a Ranger, I knew how to mask my trail in such a way that would confuse almost anyone, and I gambled on the notion that my ruse with Cyrel's body would distract them. It seems my gamble paid off, as nobody ever found me in Macadre, where I used the sword to usurp power from a feeble old man. There, I again proved my worth by raising an army, seeking out the other armor pieces, and planning my invasion. And through it all, I was left in peace by the elves, and other so-called 'noble'

races, who were too afraid to brave the lawless lands north of their
borders.

"And now, with Riorik's demise, there are only two of you standing
between me and the final pieces of armor that will ensure my absolute
victory." Shadrack ended with a wink, smiling at his captive audience.
Nordahs was immediately reminded of Ammudien's words about the
armor's safety measures, meant to prevent all pieces from being wielded
by a single individual.

The armor had been smithed as opposing pairs—the sword with the
shield, and the breastplate with the greaves. If a single individual tried to
possess both parts of a given pair at the same time, the armor would
prevent it. Nordahs realized that if Shadrack was intent on possessing all
four pieces at once, then his father must not be aware of the armor's
safety measures.

"While I disagree with your motives and purpose, I cannot deny your
position," started Nordahs as he tried to calmly address his father. "You

have the advantage, one I cannot defend against. Kirin and I will make no obstacle to you retrieving your remaining prizes. I only ask that you do not desecrate Riorik's body any further. He acted with honor and the truest of intentions. That may not be something you respect, but we do, and since we won't cause you any trouble in your retrieval of the armor, we ask that you give us that in return."

Kirin, himself unaware of the armor's built-in defense mechanism, shot Nordahs a shocked and disapproving look. Nordahs exchanged glances with the elven wizard, trying to indicate he had a plan without Shadrack picking up on it.

Thankfully, Kirin understood Nordahs' look. It was one Riorik had given him many times while they were growing up. It didn't exactly fill Kirin with a sense of comfort, but like Nordahs, he knew their options were limited. The wizard had little choice but to go along with Nordahs' plan, whatever it might be. He had to trust his friend.

Together, the two younger elves threw their hands up as a sign of capitulation.

"Lower your barrier," Shadrack demanded of Kirin.

"I'll need my wand to do that," Kirin replied. "Though it'll break on its own if enough damage is dealt to it."

"Then no wand is needed," huffed Shadrack, and he walked towards the barrier with Raiken's sword firmly in hand.

The power of the sword combined with the strength granted by the breastplate allowed Shadrack to smash through the barrier in a single blow. The transparent curtain that had protected the trio blinked and flashed as it faded away. Shadrack stepped beyond the barrier's boundary and moved in the direction of Riorik's body.

Kirin bent to pick up his wand before following after his father's murderer, but Nordahs immediately grabbed the angry wizard to delay him.

"Just wait," Nordahs assured Kirin. "Our chance will come shortly, but not yet."

Kirin still didn't know what Nordahs' plan was, but he obliged. He understood from experience the position Nordahs was in now. It was the same as what he and Riorik had endured for years. But for Nordahs, not only had his father killed Riorik's father, but he'd also killed Riorik as well. Kirin understood the struggle of emotions in Nordahs' head, torn between the joy of reuniting with his father and his anger over being abandoned. The familiar emotions compelled the wizard to trust in Nordahs' plan.

The pair watched as Shadrack approached where Riorik had fallen. Sagrim's shield still lay nearby, forgotten by everyone else in the chaos that continued to rage around them. Shadrack eagerly bent over to pick up his latest prize. But to Shadrack's absolute dismay, the shield slid out of his reach with each attempt to retrieve it.

At first, Shadrack assumed Draynard's grapple was still attached to the shield and this was just some crazed prank by someone nearby. But when Shadrack looked around, he could find no strings leading from the shield and Draynard's grapple lay on the ground near the unconscious bandit.

Confused but undeterred, Shadrack tried again to grab the shield. But again, the shield slid away. He tried a third time, and once more the shield eluded Shadrack's reaching hand. Frustrated, Shadrack drove his sword into the soft soil so he could use both hands to take what he felt belonged to him. Now, with both hands free, the elf walked towards the shield and was finally able to pick it up from the ground.

Shadrack took a moment to revel in his victory, small as it may have been. Pleased with his success, Shadrack returned to his sword. He gripped the shield with this left hand and with his right pulled the sword from its dirty container.

As soon as he pulled the sword from the ground, holding it near the shield, the armor's protective spells kicked in. The shield and sword repelled each other as far as Shadrack's outstretched arms would allow. He stood with his arms wide, but even with the additional strength from the breastplate, Shadrack could not budge his arms. The elf was stuck, unable to move, and for the first time in a long time, defenseless.

"Now!" Nordahs urged an eager Kirin.

In a frenzy, the wizard flicked his wand in the air, hastily carving out the runes of a fireball spell. As soon as the runes were complete, Kirin flung them towards the immobilized Shadrack.

The runes erupted into a searing hot fireball, flying directly at Shadrack and aiming to kill.

Shadrack knew Sagrim's shield was his only chance of survival. Though unsure of what magic prevented his movements, Shadrack instinctively dropped the sword so he could brace himself behind the shield. To his surprise, releasing the sword allowed him to control the shield once more. He'd expected the fireball to explode around the shield, but instead, the shield deflected the magic spell and sent it soaring back at its caster. Kirin was forced to quickly throw up a barrier spell to defend against his reflected spell. The wizard barely completed the spell in time to block the incoming projectile.

The fireball struck the barrier at full force, the impact shattering the wizard's defensive magic and sending shockwaves that knocked down both Kirin and Nordahs. The blast struck Shadrack too, but his enhanced strength allowed him to more easily withstand the force.

With his attackers disabled, Shadrack returned his attention to the armor. He picked up his sword again, only to immediately be returned to the same outstretched position. Finally, Shadrack realized the connection between the armor and his predicament. He would be forced to choose between Sagrim's shield or Raiken's sword. Defense or offense.

For Shadrack, the choice was simple—offense. He dropped the legendary shield, abandoning the magnificent protection it offered without a second thought. In his mind, Shadrack felt more secure with the protection of the breastplate than the shield. He decided the sword would be more useful to him in his quest for conquest.

Armed with the sword and breastplate, Shadrack could now finish what he'd started.

Chapter 12

"Traitor!" came a yell from the distance. "You murderous traitor!"

The cries drew Shadrack's attention. The elf turned to see the whole of the

Ranger Guild descending onto the battlefield.

The elves, who'd received Asbin's letter, had been watching from the

sidelines, listening to Shadrack's confession with their fine elven hearing.

Hearing the truth angered the elves. Shadrack's deceit, which caused the Rangers to mourn his death, his ploy to cast shame on Cyrel's legacy and family for a crime they didn't commit, and their failure to see through Shadrack's ruse fueled the rage of the Rangers.

Whatever their reasons, the elves of Rishdel rushed to aid their fellow defenders. Asbin's message only said that Riorik and Nordahs were helping to fight a great threat. The elders didn't know that the threat was from one of their own. Now that they'd seen the invasion was being led by Shadrack, the Rangers felt responsible.

Commander Greenblade was the most outraged of the Rangers. The veteran Ranger had been extremely hard on Riorik during his training because he thought, like so many others, that Cyrel was a traitor, not Shadrack. Knowing the truth made Commander Greenblade feel guilty and ashamed for projecting his anger at Riorik. And moreover, he would never be able to apologize to his young recruit for his less than honorable actions.

Commander Greenblade ran directly towards Shadrack, while many of the other Rangers expertly took aim at the invading archers or rushed in to help the remaining defenders struggling against the horde.

With his two-handed claymore readied for battle, Greenblade used his weapon's superior length to dispatch the horde's fighters who tried to get in his way. The expert Ranger saw the attacks coming well in advance and was able to heave his heavy weapon's blade around in time to strike down his opponents before they got too close to him.

The first opponent that made the mistake of going after Commander Greenblade was a dark elf. Greenblade swung the huge claymore around, bringing the massive sword's edge down from over his head. The weighty blade struck the dark elf from above, cleaving the his skull in two and splitting the elf's body in half as the blade continued down, cracking and splitting bones. Greenblade stepped forward between the dead dark elf's halves, surrounded by a pool of blood.

Next in his path was a bandit who thought himself better prepared. Greenblade spotted the bandit just as easily as he had the dark elf. He swirled around on his heels, holding out the lengthy blade as he turned. The bandit thought he'd be clever and try to jump over the commander's blade, but he fell for the crafty commander's feint. Commander Greenblade tilted his blade as he finished his spin, catching the bandit in mid-jump.

The blade severed the bandit's leg and sent what was left of the bandit tumbling through the air. The bandit's leg fell to the ground as nothing more than a lifeless lump. The rest of the bandit flipped and flopped through the air before crashing to the ground a second later, crying in pain and gripping his mutilated stump.

Commander Greenblade didn't bother with the bandit anymore at this point and continued towards Shadrack. Even if by some miracle the bandit did survive, he was no longer a threat to anyone.

Next up for the commander was a pair of gnolls. The hairy, over-sized dogs figured that a joint attack would be more successful after seeing what happened to the last two individuals.

Unfortunately for the gnolls, their plan wasn't much better.

The beasts agreed that they would charge the elf together, one gnoll following the other. Their idea was that if the elf managed to defend or deflect the first gnoll, the second gnoll would be too close for the elf to respond to.

What they didn't count on was the elf seeing the two gnolls charging in line.

Commander Greenblade masterfully sprinted towards the charging gnolls. The lead gnoll, seeing the commander's charge, jumped at the elf. The second gnoll followed suit. But Commander Greenblade used the long blade to stab the lead gnoll in the belly while in mid-air.

Greenblade didn't stop there though.

With the first gnoll impaled, Greenblade jumped as high as he could with the weight of the gnoll now affixed to the blade's edge, pushing his claymore's blade through the first gnoll and catching the second gnoll in mid-air.

Despite being skewered, the gnolls were still alive as the three landed back onto the ground. The first gnoll clawed and scratched at Commander Greenblade, but the more it swiped at the elf, the more it hurt itself on his blade. The second gnoll was also wiggling and writhing, desperate to free itself from the sword's edge. Panicked, the gnoll clawed his companion and pushed him down the blade's edge, causing the first gnoll's injury to worsen that much faster.

Commander Greenblade dropped his trusty claymore as the lead gnoll was getting dangerously close with its razor-sharp claws. Once the sword and gnolls were on the ground, it was only a matter of time before the foul beasts freed themselves. The veteran Ranger knew that he couldn't leave these foes just yet, but he was eager to move on quickly. Luckily, just as the commander pulled his dagger from the sheath tucked into the back of his leather leggings, two arrows screamed down from above and pierced the gnolls' hearts, killing them both instantly.

Commander Greenblade looked back to see two Rangers, bows in hand and waving him on.

Greenblade pulled his claymore from the dead beasts before returning his attention to Shadrack, who by now had also turned his attention to him.

"I mourned you!" shouted Commander Greenblade to Shadrack. "We all mourned you! How dare you play us for fools like this! How dare you make us think Cyrel had gone mad when it was really your madness that killed him! We buried you with honors!"

"He was no friend!" an angry Shadrack yelled back. "That egotistical fiend rose to the top by standing on my back! Even in death, he took honors that were mine! I did not betray him, he betrayed me! I only took what should have been mine, just as I will take what should be mine now!"

"You ignorant twit!" Commander Greenblade fired back. "Cyrel Leafwalker saved your life more times than you know. His honor was not of his making but ours. We witnessed him carry you through training and then again through the field. We were in awe that you ever achieved the rank that you did before we realized that Cyrel kept you close to him so that he could continue to look after your shortsighted self."

"LIES!" a now angered Shadrack yelled. "He purposefully kept me from rising to an equal level and getting my own command because he was afraid that without me he would be shown for what he really was—a fake! He held me down so that I could continue to grow the legend of Cyrel Leafwalker!"

"He kept you there because he knew you were not able to lead. He kept you there so he could keep you alive. If anything, Cyrel's legacy was tainted because of you. Because he risked his own reputation by convincing the elders to make you a lieutenant when you didn't deserve it. Everybody knew that it was him that secured you promotions, not the other way around. Admit it, you killed him not because he stole what was yours, but because you wanted what was his! You could never achieve the same success as Cyrel no matter how hard you tried, and that made you jealous—jealous enough to kill the one elf who called you friend. Hell, I was jealous of him too, but not fool enough to kill him simply because he was the better Ranger. You are a disgrace to elves and the Rangers Guild."

"Those are mighty words from someone who only found himself in line for a promotion in our absence," countered Shadrack. "And if I am so inept and unworthy of leading, then how do you explain this? I gathered these forces. I led them here. I conquered Kern and destroyed Dresdin. I led an army greater than all the Rangers in your beloved guild. I have faced several foes and yet here I still stand, alive. How do you explain that?"

"Your betrayal bought you a sword that cannot be contested in battle. You lead because those who follow you are afraid of your weapon, not of you. And now, now you have the breastplate, so even in your ineptness, no weapon can breach your armor. You are only alive because of your equipment, not because of your skills. If you truly think you are a great

fighter worthy of more than what you were given, then prove it. Put down

your sword, remove your armor, and fight me with honor—not with stolen

gifts and unearned respect."

"You want a chance to prove that you are the better Ranger, is that it?"

asked Shadrack. "Fine then, I'll give you that chance."

The fallen Ranger sheathed Raiken's sword.

"And the breastplate?" asked Commander Greenblade.

"This is a battlefield, so you'll have to grant me this one concession.

Removing such a significant piece of equipment is not easy nor quick. But

as it only protects my torso and arms, and you are such a great fighter

compared to my own incompetence, that should be of little concern to

you."

Greenblade and Shadrack were now in range of one another. The

commander immediately launched an attack, hoping to catch Shadrack unprepared. He swung the massive claymore, aiming to take the elf's head from his shoulders.

Greenblade's aim was on point, but his attack didn't connect.

Shadrack lifted his arm clad in the shiny green vambraces and blocked the huge weapon's path. The claymore bounced off the armor without leaving a single mark or scratch on it. The fallen Ranger grabbed the claymore's blade and, with a single tug, yanked the giant sword from the commander's hands before tossing the blade across the battlefield where it impaled one of the dwarves taking aim with his blunderbuss.

"There now, that's better," chuckled Shadrack. "Now we can see what kind of Ranger you truly are."

"Still hiding behind someone else's armor I see," countered the commander. "Only brave when you know that you have the upper hand, is that it?"

"I grow bored with your simple thoughts and insults," replied Shadrack.

Shadrack reached out to grab the other elf, but the commander was able to move away in time to avoid Shadrack's grasp.

"You may be strong, but your strength makes you slow, even for an elf," Commander Greenblade taunted as he dodged Shadrack's attempt.

Shadrack only smiled as he attempted to grab his opponent again. Once more, Commander Greenblade moved out of the way, only this time it wasn't a flawless escape.

The veteran Ranger had failed to notice the large rock behind him. As he dodged the second attack, his foot caught the rock, sending him tumbling to the ground.

Shadrack knelt by the fallen commander, grabbed him by the shoulders, and held him down, bringing to bear the strength given to him by the breastplate.

"My strength may make me slow, but at least I still see what's around me. For such a stupid, ineffective Ranger, I seem to have gotten the drop on you, haven't I?

"Go on then," Commander Greenblade started, "use a power that's not yours to take a position you don't deserve in search of praise you haven't earned. Go on then, finish me a—"

The commanding Ranger was interrupted as Shadrack slammed him into the hard, rocky surface. The repeated blows shattered the bones throughout the commander's body but didn't kill him. Shadrack wanted to make the broken and beaten commander a living example of what can happen to those who might oppose him.

Having dealt now with Riorik, Commander Greenblade, Kirin, and Nordahs, Shadrack pulled out Raiken's sword again and set about finally finishing the invasion he'd started.

The arrival of the Rangers of Rishdel signaled a turning point in the fight. The defenders were regaining control of the battlefield but Shadrack's decision to abandon the remaining pieces of armor and focus on the fight wasn't something they were preparped to contend with.

Shadrack intentionally ignored the remaining dwarves with their blunderbusses, confident that his archers would keep them occupied. The breastplate would withstand the dwarves weapons, but he also recalled that the blunderbusses used a scattershot load that could very easily penetrate the rest of his unprotected body. His archers had been all but decimated by the elven archers, but there were still a few of his men left to take on the dwarves, and a few was all he needed to keep the dwarves occupied.

The angry elf contemplated going back for the greaves but quickly remembered how the shield was repelled from him when he tried to pick it up. With the breastplate on, he thought better about trying to don the greaves as well. Shadrack was determined to take no risks at such a crucial moment. Perhaps once the invasion was complete, he would experiment with the full set of gear.

#

A groggy Kirin and dazed Nordahs sat up and tried to shake the metaphorical cobwebs from their heads. The blast wave from the exploding barrier spell had knocked the two young elves to the ground and left them disoriented. By the time they both came around, the pair saw Shadrack slicing through the defending forces with the legendary sword of Raiken as Trylon's superb breastplate absorbed blow after blow from his attackers.

A gnawing fear grew in them. The battle wasn't going to end in their favor. Riorik was the only one who'd effectively used the two armor pieces. Neither Kirin or Nordahs were sure how the armor worked, and they had no idea if they could use it to mount an effective defense against Shadrack's rage. He'd learned to use his pieces to their limits.

Riorik had still fallen, even with the power the armor bestowed upon him. Had the legends of the armor outgrown the armor's actual power? Neither Kirin or Nordahs could know that the armor was every bit as powerful as the stories and that Riorik's demise was his own doing. The armor didn't

fail the elf, his emotions had when he'd allowed Draynard to distract him.

The pair eventually decided that it was up to them to stop Shadrack

without the armor. They didn't want to become dependent the armor

when they didn't understand it. It was stained with the blood of their dead

friend, and they didn't want to add theirs to it. If they couldn't stop him

with their regular equipment, then it was unlikely, to them at least, that

the greaves or shield would make a difference.

"Kirin, can you do something about all the others out here? We'd stand a

better chance if we weren't surrounded by enemies," Nordahs prompted

his wizard friend.

"I'll do what I can," replied Kirin. "But there are still some bandits behind

the city wall. I can't do anything about them without risking collateral

damage. I don't want to bring any innocent people into this."

"Agreed," said Nordahs. "Just do what you can. I'm going after my father."

Kirin and Nordahs shook hands.

"Good luck to you," Kirin told Nordahs.

"Same to you," Nordahs replied.

The two elves nodded, knowing that there was a good chance this could

very well be the last time either of them saw the other alive.

Farewells said, Kirin and Nordahs headed off in different directions.

#

Kirin headed immediately to the few remaining mages from Mechii. The

much taller elf stood out among the gnome mages as he flung spell after

spell at the encroaching forces. The wizard used almost every type of spell

he could, knowing that it would be ill-advised to use forbidden spells

among the other mages. He kept his spells largely confined to the four

main elements, occasionally drawing on a charm spell if an enemy got too

close to their position.

Kirin's charm spells didn't last long, but they would last long enough to at

least force their attackers to move downfield from the mage's position or

force them to attack their comrades. If the charmed target was hit by anything it would break Kirin's spell, but the chaos it caused weakened the invaders and bought the mages more time.

Despite this, he still failed to get the spell off in time on every closing enemy. The gnomes weren't skilled in melee combat and were equipped with only wands and staffs. If their magic failed to stop an enemy from getting close, then it was often the end for that mage.

One by one, the mages began to fall. With each mage's death, there was that much less magic to repel the invaders or create protection spells.

More and more of the invaders were closing in to attack the mages. If things didn't change soon, Kirin and the mages would be overrun.

#

Nordahs reached for his bow. The thought sickened the young elf, but the only solution he could think of was to shoot his own father with a skillfully placed arrow. As one of the standout archers in the guild, he knew that he a good chance to land such a delicate shot. Nordahs was considering the shot before he reached for his weapon, but it was a difficult decision.

Any kind of a shot to Shadrack's torso would undoubtedly fail. Trylon's breastplate couldn't be penetrated by any conventional arrow. Maybe he could pierce Shadrack's eye, but between his constant movement and warped helm, not even Nordahs could guarantee a hit there.

Nordahs considered going for one of the major arteries running down Shadrack's thighs, but as he watched Shadrack fight, Nordahs realized that the front of the leggings were covered with metal plates that would deflect a shot from the front. He'd have to aim for the back of Shadrack's leg, the area with the least amount of armor, and the weakness that Riorik had managed to find earlier.

It was the best options that he had at that moment, But as he reached for his bow, he discovered that his bow was missing. He looked back to where he and Kirin had been knocked down. There he saw his broken bow on the ground. When he was blown to the ground it must've his back.

With his hopes for a distant strike dashed, Nordahs was now forced to consider getting in close to Shadrack. A direct confrontation had ended horribly for Riorik, a fate Nordahs hoped to avoid. The young Ranger only had his two kukri daggers with him. He could throw them at Shadrack, which would then leave Nordahs weaponless if they missed, or he could try to go toe-to-toe with a bearer of the armor as Riorik had.

As much as Nordahs didn't like it, he had no other choice. If he did nothing, Shadrack, with the power of the armor, was bound to cleave his way through everyone else who stood against him. But fighting one-on-one against Shadrack was certain suicide. He had to attack while Shadrack was distracted. It was his only chance.

Nordahs finally accepted his fate. He'd need to get up close to Shadrack if he was to have a chance of stopping his enraged and crazed father's plans for conquest. It certainly was not what he wanted to do, but Nordahs accepted that there was no other way.

The Rangers from Rishdel had done a good job of disrupting the invaders, but they now found themselves coming under fire from the bandits still within and atop Brennan's walls. The bandits didn't have siege weapons, but they were equipped with bows, crossbows, slings, spears, javelins, and even a few larger crossbows mounted like turrets that could be easily operated by two or three people. The barrage of projectiles hurled at the Rangers sent the elves scurrying for cover and struggling to return fire. The Rangers were oblivious to the larger threat approaching. Shadrack was making his way closer to their position.

Nordahs was faced with a difficult situation. The young elf would need to fight his own father to try and save those who'd condemned Wuffred to death.

Chapter 13

Kirin looked on as his enemies crept closer and closer to his position. It was clear that he and the mages were slowly being overrun. Their dwindling numbers meant fewer and fewer spells could be cast in their defense, and it was only a matter of time before the magic users met their end.

There were also fewer troops left on the field to defend the magic casters. The whole group of defenders had been divided by the invaders and the bandits. The Rangers had been forced to fall into defensive positions after coming under fire by the bandits atop Brennan's outer wall.

The casters were focused on the horde's reinforcements from Kern, while the dwarves, barbarians, and what remained of Lord Veyron's forces were focused on the horde camped outside Brennan's gate and the bandits who came to their aid.

Shadrack was now wreaking havoc across the battlefield, slaughtering anyone within his reach. He killed so indiscriminately that even some of Shadrack's own forces fell to his blade simply because they were standing too close when he swung it.

The distance and lack of coordination between the defending groups meant there were severe limitations to what each of them was capable of against the larger, more powerful forces of the invaders.

The Rangers were running low on arrows as they continued to fire at the defenders along the city's wall. Soon the elves would be forced to confront their foes in melee combat.

The dwarves no longer had time to reload their blunderbusses. The close range of their enemies forced the dwarves to abandon the weapon that otherwise evened the odds between the two forces. Now the stout dwarves also had to rely on melee combat.

The barbarians benefitted from the dwarves' weapons and the gnomes' magic earlier, but they were used to relying on melee combat. With magical aid no longer available to them, the over-sized humans were left to fight their targets head-on in what amounted to little more than a brawl.

Even Lord Veyron's remaining troops had lost their advantage. The knights on horseback had all been killed or unmounted. Those still alive were forced to fight on the ground with the others, without the speed, power, and protection of their steeds. Veyron's archers had been wiped out by the horde archers from Kern.

Many of Veyron's infantry had fallen in combat but there were those left alive to fight in close-quarters against their enemies.

The only ones who could mount any type of ranged attack or defense were Kirin and the few surviving mages. Unlike arrows, their magic was unlimited, only requiring the time to draw the runes for each spell.

But the time it took to draw the runes was a danger itself. The spells that were the quickest to cast were often the weakest, and using less powerful spells meant the opposing forces were able to get closer and closer to the mages with each attempt. The number of mages dwindled, and soon they'd be forced into melee combat, something most mages were unskilled in and none were equipped for.

Wave after wave of gnolls, dark elves, humans, bandits, wargs, and other attackers charged the mages as they made their final stand.

Kirin and the gnomes formed a half-circle with their backs to the bushes where they'd hid before. The bushes offered them some protection from a rear attack, allowing them to concentrate their magic on a smaller area.

One by one, the mages continued to fall.

There were barely enough of the gnomes to help Kirin mount a defense.

"Give me cover!" Kirin shouted at the handful of mages who still surrounded him.

The gnomes flung spells as quickly as they could.

"Whatever it is you're doing, do it fast!" barked Ammudien.

Kirin set to work preparing another barrier spell like the one he'd used earlier. The elf knew the spell wouldn't last long, especially if the shield were attacked, but it would buy the group a few extra seconds to draw better spells to force back the aggressors.

"Okay!" Kirin shouted at the mages. "Everybody step back behind my runes."

On little feet, the gnomes swiftly shuffled to get behind Kirin's protective spell. As soon as the last gnome stepped within the circle, Kirin flicked his wand with great speed and authority and the barrier shot up from the ground, enveloping the small group of casters.

Their attackers slammed into the invisible barrier, some knocked down and others only staggered back a step or two. Regardless of the impact, the barrier had done as intended by holding back the horde and giving the wizard and his allies time to think and prep more spells.

But since any magic cast from within the spell's boundaries would either reflect off the barrier or damage it, the mages could only prepare the runes in anticipation of the barrier's inevitable failure.

Unfortunately for them, the barrier spell didn't last long. The horde attackers had crowded around the protective spell and repeatedly pounded against the barrier with their fists, claws, hammers, swords, maces, and whatever else they could find. The barrier flashed and sparked with each hit. Kirin knew the spell wouldn't last much longer, but he dared not to say anything to the mages. Their heads were all down, rapidly preparing spells, and all he could do was hope they finished their preparations before his barrier disappeared.

Kirin was not that lucky.

With a final shot and a loud popping sound, the barrier shattered. To make matters worse, the sound of the protection spell being broken disrupted some of the gnomes, ruining their spells and forcing them to abandon them.

Their doom was now only a few feet away. Without the barrier's protection and the loss of the spells ruined in the process, there was no hope for Kirin and the mages.

With the barrier gone, a grinning dark elf and a gnoll approached the nearest mage, prepared to go in for the kill. The mage desperately attempted to scrawl out a quick set of runes to defend herself, but the dark elf pulled the mage's wand from her hand, disrupting the spell and leaving her defenseless. The other mages were in similar trouble.

The gnoll licked its lips, lunging forward with its mouth open and ready to clamp its large teeth around the mage's head. But before it could land its attack, the gnoll was knocked back by an unexpected force that sent it rolling across the ground, clutching its ribcage with intense pain.

A loud bleating echoed through the clearing. The attackers stopped in their tracks, startled and confused by the odd sound. The mages and their enemies turned to find the source, and all eyes landed on the shaggy, bright white ram standing between the casters and the invaders.

It was the same ram that had followed the barbarians down the mountain from Barbos. The ram moved its head side to side as if it were studying the area and locating the positions of potential threats. It seemed very unusual behavior for such an animal. Nobody knew quite what to make of it.

After an awkward pause in the fighting, the dark elf returned to attacking the small female mage. He rushed in, sword in hand and ready to attack, but again, the ram sprang towards the attacker and rammed the dark elf hard with its thick, solid horns. The dark elf's ribs could be heard cracking from the impact, followed by the thump of his body hitting the ground. The blow didn't kill the dark elf, but it was severe enough to leave him with major injuries and incapacitate him.

While the first gnoll was still recovering from the ram's blow, a second one decided the ram would be his next dinner and sprang towards the shaggy-haired sheep. The gnoll lacked the element of surprise, but oddly, the ram made no effort to dodge or defend against it. Instead, the ram simply turned toward the dog-like beast flying in its direction.

The gnoll tackled the ram to the ground, and it let out a small bleat at the collision. The gnoll wasted no time burying its claws into the ram's side while clamping down on the animal's neck with its powerful jaws and sharp teeth. The attack would undoubtedly kill the ram.

As the ram silently died, the gnoll began to emit a faint glow, growing brighter by the second. As the gnoll shone brighter, the ram faded from view, and after only a few brief seconds, the ram completely disappeared.

Meanwhile, the gnoll's glow flashed, blinding the group for a brief second. When the bright light faded, the crowd of combatants were startled to find the gnoll was there no longer. Instead, there stood the ram.

Mages and enemies alike were left stunned, confused by the mysterious exchange—all except Kirin. Only he, as the lone wood elf among the two groups, seemed to realize what had happened.

"Saire?" Kirin quietly asked, calling the spirit of the ram who was said to protect the mountains.

The ram let out a quick, short bleat, almost as if it were answering the young elf's question, despite Kirin's soft tone.

The others didn't seem to understand Kirin's reference, nor did many of them care. The horde attackers were angry with the ram for disabling two of the gnolls, while the gnomes were just thankful for the help.

Enraged, the invaders charged the ram, who defended against some but seemed mostly unconcerned. It landed a blow or two against its assailants, but whenever an attack landed that would've killed the animal, the one who struck the ram would start to glow, just like the gnoll had. The light would flash brightly again, momentarily blinding them all, only to reveal that once more the attacker had disappeared and the ram was left unharmed in their place.

The gnomes had no time to puzzle out what was happening but were eager to seize their opportunity. While the horde attackers were busy trying to kill the seemingly immortal ram, the mages busied themselves casting spells to help the ram.

Only Kirin knew the truth at that moment. Saire the ram was not immortal but was a physical manifestation of the great spirit's will. With each flash of light, the great spirit's body died, but the spirit passed to its killer's body, transforming the ram's killer into the next embodiment of Saire's spirit.

In doing so, the attacker became the vessel through which Saire's protection was provided. Gone were the killers' thoughts and desires, replaced with Saire's will to protect those who represented peace. The spirit protected the people and the land, repelling the forces that would see the land razed and the people enslaved.

The arrival of the great spirit represented a significant moment in the fight. Not only did the spirit give the defenders a major advantage, but it also meant the spirit deemed the defenders worthy of its protection.

With Saire's assistance, the mages and Kirin were able to fight back the horde attackers who had come so close to killing them. Their magic finished off several of the opposing fighters, while a constant succession of attackers killed the ram only to become the ram seconds later.

One at a time, the horde attackers were slowly transforming into their own enemies, locked in a perpetual cycle that diminished their numbers and their leached away their advantage.

Kirin looked around for the other great spirits but found no signs of them. He wondered to himself if they were out there too, and if so, would they come to the defenders' aid as Saire had.

#

Deciding how to approach his father, Nordahs opted for stealth over offense. The elf carefully avoided smaller fights with Shadrack's forces as he crept closer to his target.

But in an all-out battle, stealth was not easy to achieve. Nordahs found himself constantly having to dodge arrows fired in his direction from the city wall. His movements repeatedly drew the attention of nearby troops in the horde's infantry.

In these one-on-one fights, Nordahs was able to dispatch his foes without too much trouble, delay, or ruckus. However, as he approached their leader, more and more of the horde's attention turned to the elf as he drew a little too close to for comfort. Eventually, Nordahs found himself surrounded by enemies, more than he felt confident taking on with only his two short, curved daggers.

As Nordahs' enemies closed in around him, the elf expected to die in the next attack—a thought that was becoming all too familiar, in his opinion. But once more, death did not come to Nordahs at that moment.

Instead, the ring of attackers was broken up as Yafic and Villkir rushed to Nordahs' aid. Yafic twirled and swung his small but heavy hammer around like it weighed almost nothing. With his smaller height compared to his two allies, the stout dwarf was able to slam the hammer's blunt head into the knees of one attacker. The power of the strike shattered the bandit's knee, sending the dirty human crumbling to the ground, screaming in pain. But the bandit's screaming did not last long as Nordahs quickly reached down and slit his throat with his kukri.

Meanwhile, Villkir was able to keep several of the attackers at bay with his massive Zweihander[4]. The sword's impressive length combined with the barbarian's reach allowed him to strike his opponents well before they could reach him. The barbarian's strength allowed him to wield the heavy weapon as easily as the elves and humans did their much lighter swords. If one of the attackers attempted to approach Villkir, the large barbarian would simply swing the blade in his attacker's direction, immediately

---

[4] Pronounced "Z-why-hand-air"

causing his opponent to stop and back up before the large blade made them its next victim.

From the edge of the battlefield, the Rangers had managed to eliminate many of the archers stationed along the top of Brennan's protective wall. The remaining bandits were forced to exit the city and join their brothers-in-arms in melee combat.

The Rangers were too busy to help Nordahs, Yafic, and Villkir, who were still surrounded and had now drawn the attention of Shadrack.

The three comrades worked together to keep themselves alive. They stood shoulder to shoulder, forming a triangle to protect each other's backs. They continually rotated, watching their opponents closely and striking out in defense when necessary.

The group was hoping others would come to their aid but were unable to see what was going on elsewhere on the field. The tall barbarian was the only one who could see over the heads of those blocking his allies' view, but Villkir was too focused on the more immediate threats to assess what was going on beyond them.

Slowly, Nordahs and his two allies were making progress in thinning the herd of enemies who'd encircled them. Nordahs used his elven reflexes and agility to slice and stab at various targets, often not killing his opponent but inflicting serious enough injury and pain to force them to withdraw or think twice before attacking again.

Yafic used his shorter stature to his advantage. Their attackers easily underestimated him, mistaking his place in the triangle as an opening. The dwarf used his hammer to crush feet, shatter ribs, and in one case, dislocate a jaw.

Meanwhile, Villkir was busy keeping the majority of their horde attackers at bay. He prevented the trio from being overwhelmed all at once by sweeping his gigantic Zweihander at their foes. The blade's long reach forced the shrinking number of attackers to keep their distance, at least as long as Villkir was near their position.

The three defenders had just about evened the odds against their attackers when—to their surprise—Shadrack pushed through the crowd to stand in front of Nordahs and his allies. His own fighters fell back, some of them stumbling in their haste to get out of his way.

"You have been a thorn in my side too long," Shadrack growled at Nordahs. "This is your last chance. Join me and I will spare the three of you, or defy me and I will kill you all."

"You're not my father," Nordahs angrily replied. "You have the face of my father, but inside, you are corrupted, rotten, and false. You aren't worthy of anything you feel is owed to you. You'll have to kill me then, because I'll never support you, nor your tyranny. You seek glory and respect, but you'll only find disappointment and hate because that's all you have to offer. You are no hero. The true heroes are standing with me, not against me."

Shadrack yelled in anger at Nordahs' scathing response before attacking his son.

Yafic, knowing the power of Trylon's breastplate protecting Shadrack's body, attempted to defend Nordahs by taking a swing at Shadrack's legs with his hammer, just as the dwarf had so successfully done before—but the dwarf would not find success this time.

Shadrack, being a more veteran fighter than most of his troops and a trained Ranger, saw the dwarf's attack coming. In fact, Shadrack had anticipated the dwarf would make such an attack before ever lunging forward.

The crafty elf spun out of the way of Yafic's swing, stepping into position behind the dwarf. The elf swung his armor-clad hand down with all the power of the breastplate behind it. Shadrack's fist caught Yafic in the back, sending the dwarf flying.

Yafic hit the ground and rolled several times before coming to rest against a tree. The blow left the dwarf dizzy, disoriented, and unable to help Villkir and Nordahs.

"One down, two to go," Shadrack said laughingly, mocking the downed dwarf and turning to Nordahs with a devious grin. Shadrack swung Raiken's sword at him, the shimmering green blade headed directly at the young elf's head.

Nordahs contemplated blocking with his daggers but knew it would be a futile effort. The legendary sword would pass through the kukris like they were nothing before splitting Nordahs' skull open. All he could do was attempt to evade his father's attacks until Nordahs could find an opening to attack in return. He needed a weakness to exploit and an opportunity to do it.

Nordahs closed his eyes and jumped backward, hoping he'd moved far enough and fast enough to dodge Shadrack's blade.

"Just as I expected," Nordahs heard his father saying as he opened his eyes. To his surprise, Shadrack had moved in close, bending down before his son. Nordahs had no time to react. He was momentarily frozen with confusion as he tried to work out what Shadrack was doing.

And then it became clear. Shadrack hooked his arm around behind Nordahs' leg, pulling it forward with all his might, both natural and magical. The motion swept Nordahs from his feet and sent him crashing to the ground with a hard thud. The solid ground beneath him knocked all the air from the elf's young lungs. Winded and gasping for air, Nordahs was unable to move or defend himself as his father moved to stand over him.

Nordahs watched in horror as Shadrack raised Raiken's sword over his body and prepared to thrust the magical weapon through his empty lungs.

"You've refused me for the last time," Shadrack snarled at his son.

He thrust his arms downward, driving the sword towards Nordahs' chest. Nordahs closed his eyes again in anticipation of what was surely going to be his last moment alive.

But again, the seconds passed and Nordahs did not feel the sting of a blade. He opened his eyes in shock to see his father grappling with the barbarian.

Villkir had rushed to Shadrack's side and grabbed the elf's arms. Even with the power of the breastplate, Shadrack struggled against Villkir's natural barbarian strength.

"That's not a very fatherly thing to do," Villkir grunted as he strained against Shadrack's enhanced strength. "Somebody needs to teach you how to parent better."

"We may look alike, but this coward is no son of mine," Shadrack said as he strained against Villkir's strength.

The stand-off between the two forces of seemingly equal power lasted for several seconds, long enough for Nordahs to drag a few ragged breaths into his lungs and roll out from under the bobbing sword that locked Villkir and Shadrack in place. Neither of the two noticed Nordahs' escape.

Free from the immediate threat of death, Nordahs was now confronted with a new dilemma. Should he check on Yafic, who was still lying motionless under the tree several feet away? Or should he try to help Villkir and maybe take the sword from his father? Should he take this chance to attack—possibly kill—his own father? It was a lot for the elf to consider and almost no time to do so. Each question threw him further into turmoil, clouding his judgment and slowing his decision-making.

Eventually, the young elf settled on an answer. He would end the invasion that his father had started. Nordahs would earn the honor and respect that Shadrack sought with his single-minded greed. Even if that meant killing his own father.

Nordahs swiveled around to kneel behind Shadrack, who was too distracted trying to free his arms from Villkir's grip. The young elf immediately noticed the wound Riorik had inflicted on the back of Shadrack's leg. It amounted to little more than a flesh wound, but a deep flesh wound nonetheless.

Nordahs knew he didn't have time to study the wound or debate where the best place to strike was. He needed to strike now. Shadrack's struggle with Villkir could end at any second, closing his window of opportunity before Nordahs could act.

Nordahs slashed with his dagger's edge at the wound Riorik had given Shadrack, only in the opposite direction. The kukri dug in deep as Nordahs sliced upwards, then across in an X.

The blade was sharp, but there were a few notches and burrs along its edge from the day's fighting. The defects in the blade meant that it didn't cut cleanly, and as those damaged parts met Shadrack's leg, they tore at his flesh, causing significant pain in the process.

Shadrack howled in pain. The surge of adrenaline combined with the instinct to jerk away from the source of pain was enough to break the deadlock between Shadrack and Villkir.

Shadrack's arms jerked upwards, and the sudden change in direction caught Villkir off guard. The sword pommel crashed into his chin with the force of his own strength and the momentum of Shadrack's movement combined. Knocked from his feet by the blow, Villkir let go of the sword and flipped over backward before falling to the ground face first.

Shadrack angrily and haphazardly swung the sword of Raiken around while he fought both the pain and his instinct to drop it to clutch at his new wound. Shadrack's motions were so violent and unpredictable that Nordahs had no choice but to back away. Shadrack hopped around in pain, desperately swinging his blade around to discourage another attack and buy himself time.

After a few seconds of howling and yelping, Shadrack regained his composure. It didn't take him long to realize that Nordahs was the one who'd caused him this latest wound.

And it didn't take Nordahs long to realize that Villkir, like Yafic, was no longer in any shape to help him. Nordahs was alone against his father, a scenario that filled the young elf with dread.

But this was just the fight Shadrack had been looking forward to after Nordahs' final refusal to stand with him. He was still furious that Nordahs had refused to join his pursuit of conquest, power, and respect, even if that respect were only earned out of fear.

Shadrack moved in for the kill. He charged Nordahs as his son stood frozen with fear and sadness.

But Shadrack's charge was interrupted by a thunderous roar that echoed across the battlefield. Father and son both turned to see a huge brown bear charging through the tree line, toppling small trees that stood in its path. The large bear was headed straight for Shadrack.

Nordahs took one look at the bear's size and its thick, brown fur and immediately recognized it as Izu, the great spirit that protected the forest. Nordahs had encountered Izu before, during his hunt to gain entry to the Rangers Guild. He'd stalked Izu, not knowing the bear was the great spirit at the time, only to be saved by the bear from a pack of wolves that had been stalking him.

The bear's identity was unknown to Shadrack, who only stared at the monstrous animal charging towards him. The elf was so dumbstruck by the bear's size and sudden arrival that when Izu reached Shadrack's position, Shadrack was too slow to attack or defend.

Izu swatted Shadrack with his gargantuan paw. As the bear's forepaw

smacked the impenetrable armor, his six-inch claws raked the shiny

breastplate.

The powerful blast sent Shadrack tumbling to the ground. For the first

time in a long time, Shadrack encountered a force greater than his own.

But he was not to be outdone.

The bear may be bigger and stronger than Shadrack, but he was still

confident Raiken's sword could kill the bear just as easy as it had everyone

else who got in his way. The elf hurried to his feet and retrieved the sword

that had been knocked from his hand in the fall.

Shadrack charged at Izu. The enormous bear stood up on his hind legs,

taller than any barbarian or troll. The great forest spirit roared defiantly at

the charging elf.

Seeing the bear who'd saved his life now under attack, Nordahs threw

himself between Shadrack and Izu without hesitation. He swept his kukris

against Shadrack's legendary blade in an effort to deflect it. The kukris snapped as they struck the blade's hard edge, but it was enough to divert Shadrack's sword away from Nordahs' body and away from Izu. It was a noble move by Nordahs, but it cost the young elf his only weapons. Shadrack continued forward, missing Nordahs with his blade but ramming his son with his shoulder, knocking Nordahs to the ground one more.

"Enough of this!" Shadrack yelled in frustration. "You die now!"

Shadrack wasted no time, eager to strike down Nordahs before anyone else could come to his aid. He thrust the sword hard and fast at Nordahs' chest.

Nordahs watched the glowing green edge move towards him as though time had slowed, and suddenly everything went dark. For the span of a breath, Nordahs believed he was dead and that the darkness was what awaited him in the afterlife. But the darkness didn't last.

The darkness began to fade, and Nordahs looked at Shadrack standing over him, frozen in mid-attack. His father glowed but didn't move. The glow surrounding Shadrack seemed to get brighter as the darkness over

Nordahs lifted. A second later, the glow around Shadrack flashed, and when Nordahs opened his eyes again, he saw only Izu.

On the ground, under the enormous bear, was Raiken's sword and Trylon's breastplate. Nordahs then realized what happened.

Just before Shadrack's attack could land, Izu stepped over Nordahs. The bear's massive frame blocked out all light, leaving Nordahs in the darkness. In doing so, Shadrack's attack struck Izu, not Nordahs. Shadrack had taken Izu's life, so Izu took Shadrack's in return, just as the legend said.

The defeat and total evaporation of Shadrack sent the remaining troops of the horde fleeing in all directions. The majority of them bolted towards the river that flowed behind Brennan.

Nordahs looked at Izu and wondered if his father's soul had been fused with Izu's or simply replaced. Was there anything of his father to be found in Izu or not?

His question was put on hold as he became aware once more of what was going on around him. The fighting had largely come to an end. The young elf soon noticed Saire's presence as the ram approached. Nordahs wondered about the other great spirits. Were they nearby too?

Flashes of light could be seen coming from the direction of the river. Screams could be heard between the flashes, and moments later, the defeated horde rushed back onto the battlefield, throwing down their weapons, surrendering, and begging for protection from the spirits hunting them at the river's edge.

After questioning the surrendering soldiers, it was clear that the river exit had been guarded by Arissa and Leza, the other two great spirits. They were said to watch over and protect the land in the forms of a great lioness and large rock lobster.

With the battle won, all that was left for the survivors was to round up the defeated horde and set right what had been done to so many in the name of conquest and evil.

Chapter 14

Once the fight was over, Nordahs, Rory, Ammudien, and Kirin set about

securing the Ascension Armor, eager to keep the four pieces out of the

hands of anyone else. The breastplate, sword, and shield were scattered

around the battlefield and easily recovered, but the greaves were another

matter. They were still on Riorik's dead body, and the four friends agreed

that it would be disrespectful to strip Riorik on the field.

They circled around Riorik, and much like Nordahs and Ammudien had done for Wuffred, the group positioned their fallen friend so he laid on his back with his hands laid across his chest. They offered prayers, as was the elven tradition. Some of the Rangers who were detaining the the survivors came over to offer their own prayers for Riorik as well.

Yafic and Villkir made their way over to say their farewells to Riorik and give their condolences to the four survivors, then stepped back and let them continue grieving the loss of their friend.

Yafic and Villkir didn't get far before Nordahs excused himself from the others and hurried to join them.

"Where do you think you two are headed?" Nordahs asked the dwarf and barbarian.

"I can't say much about him," Yafic responded while pointing at Villkir, "but I have a very pregnant daughter at home that I need to return to. Someone has to tell her that the love of her life won't be coming back from this fight and won't be there to take care of her and her child. Not a conversation any parent wants to have with their child, but it has to be done."

"About that," Nordahs started. "I would like to be there to tell her myself. I was there when Wuffred died. Riorik said it was his responsibility. He thought this whole mess was caused by his father. Now that we know it was really my father, I feel the burden that once unfairly rested on his shoulders. It would only be right if I delivered that message instead of putting that burden on you."

"That is a noble offer, young Nordahs," Yafic conceded. "How about we strike a deal? You can return to Rhorm with me to tell Asbin what happened to Riorik and Wuffred, but first, you let me accompany you to Rishdel so that I can honor their sacrifice too."

The two agreed to accompany one another. Nordahs knew he had the support of Ammudien, Kirin, and Rory, but to have Yafic express his gratitude and respect for Riorik and Wuffred so openly meant a lot to the young elf. Yafic had only recently met Riorik, and all he knew of Wuffred was Asbin's condition. For him to see and understand what the loss of those two meant to the band of friends and how they were both instrumental in defeating Shadrack was most unexpected.

"I was just going to head home, but I'd also like to join you all in carrying Riorik back to Rishdel," added Villkir. "I barely knew him, but he stood tall and confronted evil, even when he thought that evil was his own flesh and blood. That took guts. Lesser folk would run and hide, but he stood tall and firm. Without his actions, more would have assuredly perished, and we may not have succeeded. He believed and fought when few others were even willing to listen. He stood up to what he knew was wrong instead of looking away or acting against his conscience. That's a life worth honoring."

Villkir's words meant a lot to Nordahs. The barbarian made Nordahs reflect on Riorik's determination and unyielding morals. He gave up his chance at redemption in the guild to abandon his post and ignore an order from the elders because he knew killing Wuffred was wrong and unbefitting a Ranger. Riorik carried on finding the armor even when he was hurt. Even after they'd met up with Kirin and thought it was Cyrel pulling the strings behind the invasion, Riorik pushed forward. And then he died confronting the elf he thought was his father and was prepared to kill him if necessary.

As Nordahs paused to reflect on the last several weeks of Riorik's life, a few tears rolling down the elf's smooth skin and high cheekbones. The Ranger found himself brought to tears at the thought of what Riorik must have felt through it all, especially after believing that it was his own father behind it all. Nordahs had only dealt with that burden for a very short time, but Riorik had to deal with it for several days. He thought he somehow knew how everything impacted Riorik when the truth was he did not, or at least not until today, and it was all a bit much for the elf.

"Thank you for seeing him the way that I do," Nordahs said to Villkir and Yafic. He choked on his emotions as he tried to hold back the tears. "Others have condemned him and chastised him for years for something that was beyond his control. I always expected the memory of his father to

be the cause of his death, and I never expected to see people willing to

honor Riorik's memory when that time came. He still has a mother in

Rishdel, you know. As much as his death will pain her, she will be pleased

to see Riorik surrounded by so many more friends than just me and Kirin.

Your respect for him will add honor to his memory. It means a lot to me,

and I'm sure it will mean a lot to his mother."

The three returned to where Kirin, Ammudien, and Rory sat offering

prayers around Riorik's body. The six allies gently lifted Riorik from the

ground and carried him to a nearby hay cart that they'd salvaged from the

battlefield. They lovingly placed his body atop the hay that filled the cart

before Villkir grabbed the cart's yoke and pulled it behind him. Together,

they turned and walked towards Rishdel with the armor and Riorik in tow.

They left the clean up to the rest. They'd all done their part, and now they

wanted to lay Riorik's body to rest with the honors he very much

deserved.

#

The surviving bandits and invaders were rounded up and secured with shackles and rope from Brennan. The population made no attempt to stop the allies from entering the city. In fact, they were quite willing to sell their ropes and shackles to the victorious army. With their prisoners secured, most of the humans, barbarians, mages, and dwarves headed with for the dungeons of Fielboro.

It was decided by Elder Bostic of the Rangers Guild and the others who'd taken charge of the clean up to keep the prisoners in the one city not affected by the invasion. Fielboro was the best city to secure those who had surrendered in until their fate was decided. Among the leaders of the victorious peoples, it was universally agreed that to keep the prisoners in any city that had lost a significant portion of its population would put the prisoners at risk of vigilante justice. Cities that suffered at the hands of the invaders or were actively involved in either perpetrating the invasion or defending against it would potentially harbor some ill-will towards the prisoners or may help them escape. Fielboro was near the southernmost coastline of Corsallis, and as such, it had been largely unaware of and unaffected by the invasion, therefore making it the safest place to hold the prisoners.

It was a marching train of people.

The prisoners were grouped and bound together with chains and rope, and each group was escorted by an assortment of defenders. It would be a long, slow march from Brennan to Fielboro given the injuries and other conditions sustained by the defenders and invaders alike, so it was decided to start marching as soon as possible. The defenders all were eager to return to their homes, friends, and family, but they all agreed that they shared a responsibility to see the prisoners safely transported and properly confined so they could face true justice when the time came. The only group to not throw their full support behind the escort effort was the elves. Elder Bostic assigned several of the lower ranking Rangers to the escort, but the remaining Rangers, including all of the guild's elders, returned to Rishdel. Elder Bostic offered no explanation for his decision, and nobody questioned it.

There was something odd about Elder Bostic's departure though, and it had many of the allies wondering. The elven leader also chose not to walk with Nordahs and the others carrying Riorik's body to Rishdel. Instead, Elder Bostic and the remaining Rangers set about collecting the elven dead that laid strewn across the battlefield and preparing to take their bodies home, per the elven traditions. But they deliberately avoided anyone tending to Riorik.

Nobody understood why. But Nordahs and his friends didn't even notice, nor did they care. They were determined to honor Riorik and Wuffred whether the rest of the guild wanted to join them or not.

#

Less than a day later, Nordahs and his friends arrived at Rishdel with Riorik in the hay cart. The Rangers guarding the gate were leery when they saw Nordahs and Kirin accompanied by a gnome, a dwarf, a barbarian, and a human. But orders had already been sent from the guild to expect the odd group, so they were let in without hassle or restriction.

Nordahs and Kirin asked the others to wait near the gate. The two elves wanted to take Riorik's body to his mother. She would have an opportunity to see her son one last time before his body was cremated in accordance with their traditions and beliefs. It was going to be a hard but necessary stop.

Plus it would give Nordahs a chance to see his own mother too, since she lived next door. He hadn't seen his mother since he and Riorik first left Rishdel after being ordered to kill Wuffred. Even when they returned to warn the elders about the invasion, Nordahs wasn't given a chance to properly visit his only relative. He desperately wanted her to know that he was safe, but also, he wanted to be the one to tell her the truth about Cyrel and Shadrack. Nordahs didn't want his mother to learn of her husband's deceit from anyone else.

Their first stop was Riorik's and Kirin's home.

Kirin knocked on the door and waited for his mother Bjiki to answer. Bjiki opened the door to see her oldest son's face. At first, she was excited to see Kirin, but the sadness on his face, especially in his eyes, told her all that she needed to know.

"Where is he? Where's my baby?" she asked with tears already in her eyes. She pushed past Kirin and moved towards the cart.

She leaned over the cart with her hands and head laying on Riorik's chest, crying over her lost child.

Kirin could do nothing but put his arm around her. There were no words he could say to relieve her pain or shorten her mourning, and he knew it. All Nordahs could do was silently watch. He wanted to be the one to tell Bjiki about Riorik's heroism and Cyrel's true legacy, but he knew that this wasn't the time to broach the subject.

After several tearful minutes and a long, emotional hug with Kirin, Bjiki wiped her eyes and looked at Nordahs.

Nordahs instantly became extremely nervous as she approached him. He wondered what she might do or say. Was she angry at him? Would she slap him? Curse him? Hug him? The terrified elf didn't know and could only wait for Bjiki to answer those questions.

"Did he find what he wanted? Did he find Cyrel?" is all she asked.

Nordahs paused to collect his thoughts. He wanted to tell her everything, but he wanted to do it delicately. He finally realized that there was no delicate way to really put it, so he just told Bjiki the truth as plainly as possible.

"He found what he needed," Nordahs started, intentionally avoiding Shadrack and Cyrel's names.

"He found his father?" Bjiki asked, confused by Nordahs' vague answer.

"He found the truth about Cyrel, but not Cyrel," Nordahs answered.

He wanted to just blurt out everything, but he was finding it more difficult to speak each time he opened his mouth. Nordahs knew that he couldn't hide Shadrack's involvement in Cyrel's death and the failed invasion, but since Shadrack was his father, Nordahs struggled to admit it.

"Nordahs," Bjiki started, "I've known you since you were born. I know when there's something you're hiding. Whatever it is, just spit it out."

Nordahs was given a brief reprieve when his mother heard Nordahs' voice and burst out of her home to see her son. She sprinted over to Nordahs and threw her arms around him. The two shared a long embrace before Nordahs pulled back slightly and told his mother and Bjiki that they both needed to hear what he had to say.

The three of them stood in the road while Nordahs explained that Cyrel hadn't murdered Shadrack but rather was murdered by him. A wave of sadness and relief seemed to wash over Bjiki while disbelief and anger washed over Nordahs' mother. She didn't understand what could've driven Shadrack to such evil.

Nordahs then told them about the Ascension Armor, how it was all real, and how the armor influenced the whole series of events that led them all to where they were in that moment. He could see there was still a sense of disbelief on the faces of the two mothers, so he led them to Riorik's body. Nordahs pointed out the green greaves that still covered Riorik's legs and the other pieces of the armor, which been hidden in the cart under the hay during the trip to Rishdel. He showed them how the sword and shield repelled each other. Nordahs also used his kukri dagger to demonstrate how the breastplate and shield were impervious to physical damage. Faced with Nordahs' proof of the armor's power, the two mothers had no choice but to accept Nordahs' claims.

Nordahs continued filling them in on the chain of events. He described how Riorik confronted who he thought was Cyrel at the time and how Shadrack's identity was revealed. Nordahs made sure to talk about how Riorik held his own against Shadrack and was only defeated when Draynard intervened.

Bjiki's emotions got the better of her when she realized that the bandit king was responsible for her son's death.

"Where's that dishonorable human? I bet he won't like it when I rip his head off! He took my son from me. I will take his head from him!" Nordahs' mother turned to console her friend and neighbor. The two, both heavy with emotions and new burdens, broke down in tears. They stood in the road crying and hugging. The scene made Kirin and Nordahs want to leave before they broke down too.

"We need to take Riorik to the guild," Nordahs softly told Bjiki as he and Kirin grabbed the cart's yoke and walked away.

The two elves returned to the gate. Then as a group they took Riorik's body to the guild. They stopped just before they entered the guild's doors so they could finally remove the greaves from Riorik's legs.

Nordahs was fearful that the guild might be take the armor from Riorik's body or that the elders may demand the armor pieces from the group. They opted to divvy up the armor among themselves to counter any demands the elders might make. Rory was given Raiken's sword. Yafic was given Trylon's breastplate. Ammudien was given Sagrim's shields. And Nordahs clung to Ailaire's greaves.

Each piece of armor was held by representatives of the races that originally made them. The only race not holding a piece were the barbarians.

"I don't get one?" Villkir jokingly asked.

"Come see me at my forge later, and I will see what we can do," Yafic said with a wink and a smile.

With the armor divided, the group stepped through the large doors and entered the guild. They were led towards the mess hall where the elders had gathered along with several senior ranking Rangers. The group barely got through the door to the large, open room before the Rangers descended on the cart and scooped up Riorik's corpse. There felt an instinctive urge to resist the taking of their friend's body away from them, but the feeling was brief. Nordahs knew that according to the traditions. It was part of the process to prepare the body for cremation quickly, so he quickly worked to calm down his allies.

Nordahs was calm, but looking at the elders and remembering their orders to have him and Riorik kill Wuffred angered the young elf. He jumped straight into berating the elders for their actions, telling them that he and Riorik had disobeyed their orders.

Nordahs was no longer concerned about being punished for disobeying orders or abandoning the guild. He'd lost two friends and had fought his own father. This weighed heavily on him, and the memory of the elders and their desire to see one Ranger killed by another, the same act that they'd laid shame on Riorik's family for, caused his outrage to outweigh his fear of punishment.

Nordahs yelled at the elders for several minutes. He expounded on Wuffred's involvement, and how his actions were as important in stopping the invasion as anyone else's. He chastised the elders for demanding Wuffred's death and called them cowards for fearing Wuffred only because they couldn't understand his potential or control him like they could others. He brought up the hypocrisy in how they shunned the Leafwalker family for Cyrel's perceived crime of killing another Ranger only to sanction the murder of a fellow Ranger.

There were a lot of gasps and shocked looks from the other Rangers as Nordahs scolded the elders for their actions, but he needed them all to know that Riorik and Wuffred were the true heroes. The young elf didn't hide the fact that Shadrack was involved, and made it known that it wasn't Cyrel that betrayed the guild.

"I am not proud of my father's actions, then or now, but I will not hide from them either. What he did to Cyrel Leafwalker and the entire Leafwalker family is something that can never be made truly right. But we can work to correct the stigma that has been falsely put upon them. And if that stigma is to be placed on me, then so be it, but just know that I will not back down, and I will not run. I stood up to evil, even when evil wore the face of my father, and I will stand up to any who think that I'm

somehow less of an elf or a Ranger because of his actions."

Nordahs' friends gathered around him to show their support and to show

the other elves that Nordahs wasn't alone. It was a symbol of unity across

the races that hadn't been seen since the Ascendant Lords ruled with their

grand armor forged from the glowing green ore.

"I can assure you," started Elder Bostic, "no shame will fall upon you or

your house, young Nordahs. Your father's actions were reprehensible, but

as you pointed out, so were our own. If we cannot act with the same

standards that we aim to hold others to, then we are no better than those

we condemn. We will honor those deserving of honor, including Hugh, I

mean Wuffred, who despite our misgivings, acted with all the honor of a

Ranger, even after the guild turned its back on him. That is true honor,

putting your life in danger to protect those who would likely not do the

same. His actions will not be forgotten."

"We will hold a ceremony to honor our fallen in the coming days," Elder Bostic continued, now addressing the whole room, "but first, a few of us must journey to Fielboro to see to the judgments against those who brought war to the land."

With that, Elder Bostic shook hands with Nordahs and his companions, thanking each of them for their efforts and sacrifices. Once he'd addressed each of them, Elder Bostic left the mess hall and headed off to Fielboro. The other Rangers took the elder's queue and began filing past Nordahs and the others, shaking their hands and expressing their gratitude and condolences before leaving the hall.

It was a relief for Nordahs to see the show of support from his fellow elves and Rangers. He'd been afraid that they would shun him like they had Riorik now that they knew the truth about Shadrack.

"I guess we should leave for Rhorm now," Nordahs said as he turned towards Yafic.

"Nay," replied the dwarf. "We came to honor Riorik and Wuffred with you. If the ceremony is in a few days, then we will wait a few days. My daughter is only pregnant. She'll still be there when we get back. We can tell her then not only how they died but also how they were honored. I think she'll understand and appreciate that."

Nordahs smiled at Yafic. It was a great relief to know that Yafic didn't expect him to miss the ceremony and that he'd intended to stay for it as well. Nordahs' smile only grew as Ammudien, Rory, and Villkir all expressed similar sentiments. They were all staying to see Riorik's memory and sacrifice honored in the elf's home.

#

A couple of days later, the convoy of prisoners along with their escorts arrived in Fielboro. The people of the city had heard of the invasion, mainly due to Riorik's insistence that the guild send out birds to warn the other cities. So when the convoy arrived, they were initially met by the armed forces of Fielboro, who quickly realized that this wasn't an invading force at their doorsteps.

The city's leader, Lord Senna[5], agreed to house the prisoners in his city's dungeon while they worked to come up with the crimes the invaders and bandits would be tried for. There were those who called for their immediate beheading while others wanted to show more compassion by suggesting either exile or lifelong imprisonment. It wasn't something that would be decided quickly or easily. The matter would test the uneasy and still fledgling alliance that'd been renewed between the races.

The prisoners were crowded into the small cells of the dungeon. All except one, that is.

Draynard, the King of the Bandits, the former leader of Brennan, was given a cell to himself, away from the others. To some of the other bandits, this was a sign of the great respect their captors had for their fallen leader. To

---

[5] Pronounced "Sin-uh"

the others, they were insulted to be crammed in like animals while he was seemingly left to live in prosperity.

The reality was, the allies were concerned about keeping Daynard with the other prisoners. Draynard had inspired those who followed him to fight with the invaders. There was a very real possibility that Draynard might organize some type of rebellion or escape attempt if he was allowed to have contact with or be confined with the others. Lord Senna was adamant that no possibility to threaten the lives of the guards and potentially all of Fielboro's citizens be presented to his wayward relative. Draynard's seclusion was the only condition Lord Senna required in his agreement to house the prisoners.

But seclusion did little to prevent Draynard from making attempts to find his freedom in the days following.

"I demand that you release me at once! I am the king of all humans. I am King Draynard! You cannot detain me like this," shouted an angry Draynard.

"I am your king! As your king, you must release me!" Draynard continued to shout at the guards standing watch.

As he continued to yell, a robed figure moved from the shadows to stand at his cell door. The robe's hood and the flickering lights of the wall torches hid the mysterious figure's face from view, but they did nothing to hide or distort the words they spoke.

"You are not king. You were merely a pawn that was played by an angry, vengeful, manipulative elf."

"That's not true!" Draynard shouted in rebuttal.

"Oh, but it is. The stories about your family are true. You are but the bastard child of a whore and a disgraced prince. Lord Veyron was never more than a distant cousin to the king's family, but since his family had ruled Tyleco for so long and gained so much wealth in that time, they felt they were better suited to be the royal family than an actual true heirs. Shadrack told you what you wanted to hear to woo you into doing his dirty work for him. Had he won the fight, he would have undoubtedly killed you before you ever sat upon the throne."

"That can't be true. How do you know these things if my own people have forgotten them?" Draynard demanded to know.

The hooded figure slowly reached up and pulled back the cover to reveal his face. It was Elder Bostic from the Rangers Guild.

"My dear Draynard, you forget that we elves live much longer lives than you humans. We can easily live several human generations in one lifetime. The young elves that stood in opposition to Shadrack may have looked like little more than children to your eyes, but I assure you, they were decades older than you. They are young for elves but old in the terms of every other race that inhabits this great land. Our history is remembered for ages before becoming myths, legends, and rumors. So old elves like myself remember the things that your race would have long ago forgotten or stopped believing."

"If that is the case, then who is the true king?" Draynard asked, still defiant and unwilling to accept Elder Bostic's words.

"Why, who else but the one who sits upon the throne here in Fielboro," Bostic replied.

"But none sit on the throne in Fielboro. The throne has been abandoned for generations," Draynard countered with a puzzled tone and matching expression.

"Exactly," responded Elder Bostic. "The throne has been empty for so long that the dynasty has been broken. Any member of the royal family need only to sit on the Fielboro throne, claim its authority, and ascend to the rank of King. Why, even by humanity's own customs, if someone popular enough, even if not of royal lineage, were desired by the people, then even they could be crowned king after such an extended interregnum."

"Then I claim the throne as my own!" Draynard shouted excitedly. "There, now I am the king, and I demand that I be released immed—"

"Nice try," interrupted Elder Bostic, "but I said you had to sit on the throne *and* claim the authority. Anybody can say that they want to be king, but that's not enough. It only works if you're a member of the royal family and sitting on the throne at the time you claim the authority. Or your race could raise you up to that position of their own accord, but we know that isn't going to happen. You and your ancestors are so concerned with being recognized by one another as the rightful heir that none of you realize that the throne can be claimed by any of you."

"But now you have proven yourself unworthy of the throne by throwing your support behind an ally that would prefer to see us all enslaved or slaughtered. That is not the heart of a king, but the heart of a fool. And since Lord Veyron and Lord Shiron are dead and you are unworthy, that leaves the last remaining member of the royal line, Lord Senna, as the heir apparent. He will be given the crown in a coronation ceremony in the coming weeks, though I doubt that you will be around to see it."

"So, my fate is already sealed?" Draynard asked sarcastically, assuming his question to be rhetorical.

"Your fate is not yet determined, but I can only imagine the level of anger and hatred that will go into that decision. You so readily engaged in open warfare against your own people and only so you could achieve power under the reign of a foreign ruler. That is a betrayal that I am sure will not sit lightly with the human delegates that will decide your fate. Most races tend not to be forgiving towards those who try to kill them or conspire with others to see them killed. At this point, I think the best you can hope for is a quick death. That would be far better than some of the other punishments that have been mentioned since my arrival here this morning."

"How much longer must I wait to learn my fate then?" Draynard asked with a discernable shift in his tone. His defiance was giving way to defeat.

"I'm not sure exactly when, but soon. I am here as part of the Elven delegation. We are negotiating the terms of the trials so that we can conclude this whole affair sooner rather than later. It is nobody's desire to

drag this out longer than is necessary."

Chapter 15

A few days later, the time came to honor the fallen Rangers at the guild.

Yafic, Rory, Ammudien, and Villkir had all stayed in Rishdel with Nordahs

and Kirin so they could attend the ceremony out of respect for Riorik and

Wuffred. The villagers were civil, but there was an air of uneasiness that

followed them wherever they went.

Rory and Yafic had stayed with Nordahs. His mother was grateful for the company. She was pleased to have Nordahs home, but there was an obvious sadness in her eyes when she talked with her son. When Nordahs was busy with his Ranger duties, she would talk with the human and dwarven visitors, which was a welcomed change for her.

For years, she'd believed her mate had been murdered, and then she'd spent the last several weeks unsure about the fate of her only son. Now Nordahs' mother had learned that her mate was not only alive but had done unspeakable things, including trying to kill their own child. There were a lot of emotions and thoughts she needed to express but could not bring herself to say to her son. She found it easier to open up to the two outsiders.

Meanwhile, Ammudien and Villkir stayed with Kirin and Bjiki. Riorik's mother, Bjiki, had a lot of questions for Ammudien about his adventures with Riorik. The gnome regaled her with the story of how they met, Riorik's near-death experience with the bandit's poison, his bravery at the oasis, and most of all, with an account of Riorik's absolute faith in his

father's redemption and Riorik's refusal to believe that Cyrel had been

capable of the things he'd been accused of doing.

Ammudien's description of Riorik's faith in his father filled Bjiki with pride.

She'd raised Riorik on stories of Cyrel's noble and heroic achievements.

She hadn't wanted him to think of his father as a monster, but as a good

elf and honorable Ranger. To hear that Riorik had refused to give up on his

father, even when they all thought Cyrel was behind the invasion, warmed

her forlorn heart.

It was very much what the grieving mother needed at that moment.

One morning after their return, the village bells rang throughout the town.

It was a summons for the villagers to assemble in the Guild's great hall, the

only place in the village that could accommodate everyone at once.

Nordahs, Kirin, Bjiki, and the others all filed out of their homes and joined

the other elves and visitors in the great hall.

As soon as they walked in, Nordahs noticed three new banners hanging from the rafters. Banners were hung to honor the heroes of the guild, representing fallen Rangers of years past. The three new ones, with their dark green material and gold lettering and borders, hung directly in the center of the hall. It was the highest honor to have a banner hung there. Nordahs' gaze fell on the banner in the middle, the biggest of the banners, which bore Riorik's name. Tears formed in Nordahs' eyes as he understood the significance of its size. It was was the biggest banner in the hall. The guild had elevated Riorik above all others. The young elf had gone from the most hated elf in all Rishdel to the most honored and revered.

Bjiki, who was standing between Nordahs and Kirin, broke down in tears at the sight. At first, Nordahs thought it was because she too realized Riorik's banner was the largest, but he soon discovered there was more to it than that.

"Look, Kirin," she said between the tears while pointing to the banner hanging next to Riorik's.

Kirin and Nordahs were so moved at seeing Riorik's banner that they'd not yet noticed the name emblazoned in the same gold lettering on the one next to it—Cyrel.

After discovering the truth of what had happened to him in the forest, the guild elders unanimously agreed that Cyrel, a hero in his own right for his accomplishments and service to the guild before his death, should be given the proper honors a Ranger of his significance was owed.

Ammudien then drew Nordahs' attention to the third banner that hung on the other side of Riorik's. It listed Wuffred's name. Not Hugh, but Wuffred. The Rangers had honored him in two ways with that one symbol. It was unheard of for a non-elf to be given such an honor in the great hall, partly because non-elf Rangers were extremely rare, but also that they used his real name. The banner was a real attempt to honor the berserker who the guild had previously abused and conspired to kill.

The bottom of each banner was still shrouded, indicating there was still something left to reveal. The covers would be removed as part of the ceremony to come.

Once everyone had made their way into the hall and found a seat, the elders took center stage and began a series of speeches about the losses both the guild and the village suffered in defense of their people. Family members of those who'd perished were provided a small banner to hang in homes in memory of their loved ones, along with any personal objects that had been stored in the guild.

When Elder Bostic got up to give one of the final speeches, Nordahs felt the weight of the ceremony the most. Elder Bostic talked about Cyrel, both his accomplishments as a Ranger and the unjust way in which he was vilified. Elder Bostic issued a formal apology to Bjiki and Kirin for the guild's handling of Cyrel's disappearance. He spoke for several minutes about how Cyrel was more deserving of honor in the great hall than many of those who'd come before him and that he should be a Ranger who

current and future Rangers aspired to be like.

At the end of Elder Bostic's speech, the curtain dropped away from Cyrel's

banner, revealing the words embroidered across the bottom in gold

lettering.

"A better elf than this is hard to find."

It was an obvious reference to the numerous good deeds Cyrel had

achieved in life and his devotion to his people and the guild. Even when he

held the legendary sword in his hands, Cyrel wanted to give it to the elders

so it could benefit everyone instead of keeping the power for only himself.

The words were true—it would be difficult to find an elf as great as Cyrel

Leafwalker.

Next, Elder Bostic spoke of Wuffred. In a surprising turn of events, he

openly admitted that he and the other elders had asked for Wuffred to be

killed, but Bostic was quick to condemn their act as a mistake the guild

would never repeat. He extolled the virtues of Wuffred's personality, talking about how Wuffred died to save the very people who'd wanted to see him dead.

Elder Bostic revealed that Wuffred's devotion and sacrifice had opened the eyes of the elders, and they'd now decided to open the doors of the guild to anyone, to every race, male and female alike. It was a stunning announcement to the elves especially, who'd never known a female Ranger of any race.

Just as with Cyrel's banner, when Elder Bostic finished with his speech, the cover along the bottom of Wuffred's banner was dropped to display its text.

"He died for us, not because of us."

The words echoed Elder Bostic's sentiment. Wuffred had fought to save the lives of everyone in Rishdel and beyond, even though he was perhaps the most hated person in Corsallis due to his so-called curse.

Finally, Elder Bostic spoke about Riorik. He talked about Riorik's unyielding faith in his father, his determination to become a Ranger even though nobody wanted him there, and his unbreakable spirit.

The old elf explained that he knew little about Riorik since Riorik left the guild so soon after joining, but he saw in retrospect that Riorik upheld the morals of the guild better than even the elders had by leaving and refusing their order to kill Wuffred.

Elder Bostic heaped praise on Riorik for the young elf's courage in returning to the guild and facing punishment for abandoning his post just so that he could warn everyone about the invasion. Elder Bostic compared Riorik to Cyrel, telling Cyrel's spirit that he should be proud of Riorik for never giving up, even in the face of adversity that followed him from birth to death. The guild elder praised Bjiki for raising such a great, upstanding Ranger when the odds were against them.

But the biggest praise came when Elder Bostic personally walked to the

rope hanging from Riorik's banner and pulled it to reveal the final line of

his memorial.

"He gave all so we could have some."

Unlike with the other two banners, Elder Bostic felt compelled to explain

Riorik's epitaph.

"This young elf was willing to sacrifice his home, his family, his position, his

dreams, and even his life so that the rest of us could live our lives without

fear and one day achieve our dreams. Many of us will never know the

difficulty of making such a sacrifice, and that is because he made it for us.

Riorik Leafwalker is a hero of the highest order, and though his deeds as a

Ranger are few, he will forever be remembered as the hero who died to

save us all."

The hall erupted in a deafening roar of clapping and hooting as everyone

celebrated Riorik's honor. Everyone but Bjiki, Kirin, and Nordahs, who could only cry with tears of joy, knowing that those deserving of honor finally got it.

As Nordahs and his mother prepared to leave the great hall, they looked to the rafters where Shadrack's banner had once hung. The banner was nowhere to be found. Neither of them really expected to see it there, but it was still difficult to come to terms with. Seeing it gone made the whole thing that much more real for them.

Later, they would receive the banner from the guild to keep in their home in honor of Shadrack's past service, with the condition that it was not hung publicly. The elders didn't want to honor Shadrack given his vile misdeeds, but also they didn't want their actions towards the Leafwalker family to be unnecessarily cruel.

After the ceremony had ended, Nordahs told his mother goodbye and reminded her that he had business to attend to in Rhorm. She was upset that her son was leaving so soon but knew why it was important for him to accompany Yafic to the dwarf's home.

Ammudien insisted that he also join them, but Villkir and Rory, neither of whom knew Asbin nor Wuffred well, opted to return home but vowed to stay in contact.

#

"Where are you off to now?" Elder Bostic asked Nordahs as he, Ammudien, and Yafic approached the gate to leave Rishdel.

"There's another member of our party who we need to visit. She doesn't yet know of Riorik or Wuffred's passing, and I feel I owe it to her to bring that message in person," Nordahs answered.

"That is a very noble gesture. I would expect nothing less. But I assume you'll be returning to Rishdel soon, right?"

"I would like to return to Rishdel, yes," the young elf replied. "I would like to return to the guild if you'll still have me. I know we defied orders, but I would still like to carry on the legacy of my friends if possible."

"The guild wouldn't have it any other way, Lieutenant Bladeleaf," Elder Bostic said, revealing a promotion for Nordahs.

"You have proven yourself to be every bit as great of a Ranger as Riorik and Cyrel," Elder Bostic continued. "The guild would only do itself a disservice by refusing someone who embodies the very principles we stand for to find a home among our ranks. We were wrong before. What was asked of you and Riorik should've never been. Return to the guild free of judgment and help make sure we never become that which we've vowed to defend against."

"And the greaves?" Nordahs wearily asked.

Elder Bostic grinned, understanding the young elf's underlying question. "Keep the greaves. You have well earned them. You know, the elder council was formed during Ailaire's time. He didn't want to be burdened with rulership, so he formed a committee to rule by consensus. But he kept the greaves to protect us in times of need. We would be honored if the greaves stayed in the Bladeleaf house, passing from generation to generation with the title of Protector of Rishdel. The council has already drafted an official decree to ensure that nobody can ever take the greaves from the Bladeleaf house in future."

Elder Bostic handed Nordahs a scroll with the council's decree written on it, declaring the greaves as the Bladeleaf family's property and even officially changing the name from Ailaire's Greaves to 'The Ascendant Armor of House Bladeleaf'.

"And, you know, possession of the greaves comes with a seat on the council," added Elder Bostic. "I expect you to help guide us and keep us from repeating our mistakes from the past."

Nordahs could only nod his head. He tried to speak but found himself in a state of shock, so no words came out. Elder Bostic recognized the expression and took Nordahs' hand to shake it, knowing that Nordahs would return and help lead not only the Rangers Guild but the whole village of Rishdel.

"Stay safe, Protector of Rishdel," Elder Bostic said as he motioned for the gates to be opened. "We will await your return."

\#

Days passed before Yafic and his companions arrived back in Rhorm. They walked from Rishdel to Tyleco with Rory and Villkir, where Rory helped them to secure transport to Barbos and Rhorm. But even with the transport, it was still a long and bumpy ride from Tyleco to the southeastern tip of the continent where Rhorm stood.

The dwarven city wasn't ringed with walls and gates as other cities. The dwarves lived in caves and subterranean homes with doors poking out of the surface. The mountainous terrain that surrounded the city offered a lot of natural protection, so much so that for centuries nothing else was ever needed.

Yafic's home was at the base of the mountains near the rear of the town. He led them to a door set in the side of a small grassy hill that sat atop the underground house. Beside it stood a workshop. The forge and furnace puffing smoke made it obvious that Yafic was a blacksmith. His anvils and hammers were lined up around the shop's walls, and various goods hung up as examples of his work.

But the trio weren't there to talk about Yafic's skill with a forge and hammer. They were there to see Asbin and deliver their mournful news. Yafic opened the door to his home but froze in surprise at an unfamiliar sound. The trio stood in the doorway listening for several seconds before they realized it was the sound of a baby crying.

Asbin had been pregnant when Yafic left Rhorm, but in the many days since then, she'd apparently given birth.

Yafic rushed into his house and down the stairs to check on his daughter and greet his grandchild. He didn't wait for Ammudien and Nordahs. His excitement and concern made the dwarf completely forget about his companions.

Nordahs and Ammudien just exchanged looks and shrugged their shoulders before following in Yafic's footsteps into the house.

Once inside, they found Asbin resting comfortably in her bed with the baby in her arms. She was overjoyed to see her father return but was immediately concerned by his wounds. Though some had healed since the battle ended, he'd received several cuts, including a deep one to his face that she knew would scar. Asbin tried to ask her father about his injuries, but he brushed her concern aside.

"That's nothing to worry about, my dear," he said. "Tell me about this precious child."

"Meet your granddaughter," she said, holding the small child out for Yafic to see and hold.

"And her name?" Yafic asked instinctively.

"Wuffred and I will pick a name together," Asbin replied.

Her words instantly removed the exuberance from Yafic's face. The joy of seeing his granddaughter was replaced with the sadness of what was to come.

"My daughter," he started, "there's someone here to see you."

Asbin's excitement rose, assuming Yafic was referring to Wuffred. She sat up in bed as Yafic moved out of the way to reveal only Nordahs and Ammudien waiting to see her.

Asbin's face was at first one of confusion. She didn't immediately comprehend the significance of their presence and the absence of Wuffred and Riorik.

Nordahs and Ammudien remained silent. They looked at Asbin briefly but hung their heads in grief. Neither of them could bring themselves to say the words, but their expressions told the new mother all.

At first, Asbin was filled with disbelief. She refused to accept that Wuffred wasn't there because something had happened to him. Then her disbelief turned to anger. She demanded to know where he was.

"You tell me where he is right now!" she yelled at Nordahs. "But don't you dare tell me he's dead! That's not funny!"

"I'm sorry, Asbin," were the only words Nordahs could utter in response.

It took a few minutes for her anger to subside. When it did, Asbin's emotions turned to sadness and she began crying uncontrollably. Yafic, Nordahs, and Ammudien rushed to her side, offering her their support and condolences.

Eventually, she managed to ask Nordahs what happened. He recounted the events from the oasis, taking care to describe how bravely Wuffred helped Riorik and fought their then-unknown opponent. Nordahs' voice shook with pride and grief as he explained that Wuffred's sacrifice was the only reason Riorik survived the fight.

Asbin looked up, wiped away her tears, and realized that Wuffred wasn't the only one missing.

"Where's Riorik?" she asked with deep concern in her voice.

Initially, she looked to Nordahs for an answer, but the elf broke down at the thought of his fallen friend. The answer instead came from the less emotional gnome.

"He survived the oasis and was instrumental in Shadrack's final defeat," answered the mage.

"But...?" asked Asbin, even though she'd already worked it out for herself.

"But while he was confronting Shadrack, Riorik was ambushed by one of Shadrack's allies. The ambush put Riorik in a two-against-one scenario, with none of us close enough to aid him. Those odds created an opportunity for Shadrack to strike him down."

"So, Riorik still died. Wuffred's death was for nothing," Asbin lamented. Her words stung Nordahs, but he knew she was grieving the loss of a loved one just as he was, so he didn't take it to heart.

"Actually, darling," Yafic said into the brief silence, "Wuffred sacrificed his life so that Riorik could rally others to their cause. And Riorik sacrificed his life so that you could give life to your precious daughter. Neither death was for nothing. You have every right to grieve but no reason to be angry. They died so that we may live."

Nordahs found his words again and followed up Yafic's profound wisdom with the last of their tale. He gave Asbin descriptions of how Riorik mourned Wuffred's death, the burden and regret Riorik had carried, knowing he'd have to tell Asbin what happened, and how Riorik had fought relentlessly to save the decent people of Corsallis even when he thought his enemy was his own father.

At this point, Asbin took the baby back from her father and asked to speak with Nordahs alone for a few minutes. Yafic and Ammudien didn't protest her wishes, clearing the room without question.

"I know it's difficult to learn that your daughter's father will not be here to see her grow—" Nordahs started once they were alone.

"No, I know coming here to tell me this was not easy for you," Asbin interrupted. "I'm sorry for my outburst. I didn't mean to belittle you or Riorik's sacrifice. You two saved me when I needed saving and fought for me without really knowing me. I think a lot of it is that I'm angry with myself for not being there to fight alongside you all. If I'd been there, then maybe Wuffred and Riorik wouldn't have needed to die. Maybe I could've done something to save them."

"No," replied Nordahs, "you were right where you needed to be, Asbin. I was there when both of them fell, and believe me, there was nothing any of us could've done to intervene. We would've only lost our lives along with them. No, they died so we didn't have to, and I think they knew and accepted that."

"Well, I don't think I'll ever be able to not think about that," Asbin countered. "I think that thought will always in the back of my mind. What could I have done if I had been there? How different would things be if I hadn't returned to Rhorm, you know?" Asbin pondered.

"Yeah, something tells me that I'll have similar questions myself," agreed Nordahs. "But we shouldn't focus on that. We should focus on what lies ahead. You can return to the temple and rejoin the priestesses, right?"

The mention of her former life as a priestess came as a bit of a surprise to Asbin at first, but then she remembered Nordahs had been traveling with her father, who loved to brag about her achievements.

"Priestess, huh? So my father told you about that, did he?" she remarked humorously. "Sadly no, that life is closed to me now."

"Because you left to seek the armor to spare Arala from the task?" asked Nordahs curiously.

"No, my absence has nothing to do with it. It's because of my child. Priestesses of the temple are expected to remain pure. Having a child, especially with an outsider like Wuffred, has forever closed that door to me, even if there weren't a more serious matter to prevent my return."

Nordahs' started in sudden concern.

"What do you mean 'a more serious matter'? Is there something wrong? Is there anything we can do to help?" Nordahs asked eagerly.

"There's nothing you or anyone else can do," Asbin answered. "That's actually why I asked to speak to you alone. I can't bear to tell my father about it yet."

"What is it?" Nordahs asked, anxious to know his friend's problem.

"I've lost my connection with the magic," Asbin somberly replied. "And I don't understand why. As my pregnancy progressed, I felt my magic surge. At times, it almost felt uncontrollable. But as soon as I gave birth, that connection was disappeared. I haven't felt the magic since then."

"Perhaps the delivery was just more exhausting than you'd expected? You just need some rest. Once you regain your strength, the magic will return," Nordahs tried to reassure her.

"I would love for that to be true," Asbin started to reply, "but I think it's more serious than that. I don't know if the gods have stripped me of my gift because of my child or if this is normal. Most who bear the gift as I did are sent to the temple where they remain until death, never knowing the touch of another, let alone having a child. So my situation is a bit unprecedented. But I'm afraid to tell too many people here because I have no wish to be judged or made an outcast, and I don't want my child to be blamed for something beyond her control."

"I can certainly understand that," said Nordahs. "But if they all know you had the gift before, then it's only a matter of time before others learn it's gone. I can't tell you what to do, but I can advise you to prepare for the inevitable.

"In the meantime, since the temple is no longer an option, what will you do now?" Nordahs asked, trying to change the subject.

"Arala will need help running the forge. I will apprentice with her."

"What about your father? Will he not continue running the forge?" Nordahs asked, confused by Asbin's statement.

"Father has been taking less and less responsibility in the forge of late. He's growing old. His joints ache, and without my gift to help him, I fear he'll soon be unable to work the forge at all, especially with his latest wounds. He's taught Arala well, so I have no doubt she'll excel in his stead.

He can continue to supervise the forge, but Arala and I will help. I want to stay close to home and raise my daughter."

"Do you think she'll inherit your gift?" Nordahs asked.

"It's hard to say," Asbin answered. "Most dwarves don't show any attunement with magic until their teenage years. There's something about that period when their bodies change and prepare for adulthood that makes the magic reveals itself to those with the connection. It'll be a while before we see if she has the gift."

The two continued to chat for a few more minutes. Asbin asked Nordahs to keep her secret for her a little longer but assured him that she would tell Yafic soon. They agreed that she'd been bombarded with enough stressful news lately that she could wait a few days before confronting another difficult topic. When that was settled, they decided to let the others back into the room.

Nordahs and Ammudien stayed overnight, visiting with Yafic, Asbin, and Arala. The following morning, the pair prepared to leave. Ammudien was ready to return to Mechii, and Nordahs felt obligated to return to Rishdel sooner rather than later to begin fulfilling his role as the Protector of Rishdel.

Before they left though, Asbin asked for everyone to gather around the table for an announcement.

"First, I would like to express my sincere and deepest gratitude to Ammudien and Nordahs for coming here. I'm sure bringing such news in person is not easy and it would've been easier to simply send a letter. I appreciate you traveling so far to tell me what happened to our friends. It reaffirms for me that there's good out there and that there's hope for our people to work together again, like in the old days."

"But before Ammudien and Nordahs leave, I would like to share with you all the name I settled on for my daughter last night. I thought about Wuffred and Riorik, what their lives meant for all of us, and how I could keep their memories alive, even here where many never knew their names. In the end, I decided the best way to keep their memories alive with me, and here in Rhorm, was to name her Wufrika[6], part Wuffred and part Riorik. I will never be able to call her name without remembering those who died so that she and I could live."

A few tears, a few kind words, and several hugs and handshakes later, Nordahs and Ammudien walked out the door and into Rhorm. The pair of friends made their way to the stables, where they hired two carriages to take them to their homes.

Ammudien and Nordahs said their farewells. Nordahs made Ammudien agree to send word to him in Rishdel of how the gnome got along back in Mechii. Ammudien relented on the condition that Nordahs stay in touch with him too.

A few minutes later, the carriages were ready. Nordahs and Ammudien each climbed aboard and took their seats before setting out on the paths that would separate the two friends for the last time.

#

---

[6] Pronounced "Woo-frick-uh"

Ammudien's carriage arrived in Mechii a short time after leaving Rhorm. The mage didn't know what to expect when he returned. He had left Mechii and the Mage Academy in a cloud of mockery. He'd been laughed out because he'd believed in the armor that everyone else now knew to be very real as well. Would he be honored? Would he continue to be ridiculed? Or something in between? Ammudien didn't know and was a little scared to find out.

The Flickerspell family name garnered him some tolerance from others, and in some cases, a modicum of respect, but would the realization of the armor's existence and Ammudien's part in stopping the invasion influence how the other gnomes addressed him now?

The gnome's questions were answered almost immediately after exiting the carriage.

A few gnomes who'd been moving about near the stables looked to see who was getting out of the carriage. Ammudien was instantly recognized, and the gnomes were sent scurrying about.

"It's him! Ammudien's here!" shouted one gnome as she ran towards a
nearby house.

"He's back! Someone send word to the academy! Master Flickerspell is
back!" another gnome shouted to someone in the distance before running
off deeper into the city center.

"Ammudien has returned! Hey, everybody, Ammudien has returned!"
another yelled as he ran from door to door, banging to alert anyone inside
to Ammudien's presence.

It didn't take long for the whole city of Mechii to descend on Ammudien's
position. The sudden appearance of so many gnomes, many of whom
hadn't always addressed Ammudien with much kindness, frightened
Ammudien a bit at first. But his fears were misplaced. The throngs of
people weren't there to jeer or deride the returning gnome but rather to
offer their thanks and praise.

Everyone seemed to want to shake his hand and ask questions about the armor. He smartly chose to keep Sagrim's shield hidden. Showing off the shield at a time like that would've likely caused a stampede.

Slowly, Ammudien made his way through the crowd, shaking hands and answering questions as he went. It was a very surreal experience for the gnome. When he left Mechii, Ammudien had dreamed of returning home to such a grand welcome, but he never really thought it would come true. Eventually, the mage made his way to his family home. It was a large stone structure with spires topping its many towers. He hadn't seen any of his family in the crowd or anyone from the key houses that oversaw Mechii's daily operations. As he entered the door to his home, he discovered why. Every gnome of influence and power in Mechii had gathered in the Flickerspell family home to await Ammudien for a private conversation. The conversation was very political and serious in nature, much to Ammudien's annoyance. His time with the allies had shown him that things can be discussed and decided with much less formality and protocol than those from Mechii had grown accustomed to. Ammudien managed to slog through the formalities of the discussion until they reached the main reason for meeting with him.

Those who governed the Mage Academy offered to forgive Ammudien's previous trespasses in exchange for his services defending the city. In addition, they told Ammudien that they would allow his return to the academy as a student on the condition that he shared his knowledge of the armor with them.

Ammudien politely declined their offer.

"You have some nerve to 'forgive' me for having a belief in something that turned out to be real when you refused to acknowledge it until it was used to save your precious academy. And while I know there's still more for me to learn, I think I've proven myself more capable than your average student."

The council members looked at Ammudien with disbelief and shock at his denial of the academy's offer.

"Well, perhaps this conversation is best left for once Ammudien has had some rest. He's been through quite an ordeal. I think we can all agree on that," Ammudien's aged father interjected, trying to diffuse the tense situation.

"That's all right," countered Ammudien. "My opinion won't change with sleep. But I'll offer the academy this instead. I'll return to the academy, but not as a student. Nor will I be a teacher. I will return in the capacity of a senior researcher, where I'll be left alone to research whatever magical topics I choose, on the condition that my efforts and findings are shared with the academy and to the benefit of us all."

"But such research is left to the White Robes," one of the other gnomes said. They were the highest-ranking mages in Mechii, and were the only ones allowed to wear robes of pure white.

Ammudien just smiled, knowing that his offer required that he be given that right, which was his dream.

"And what of the armor? Do the elves still possess our ancestor's piece?" another of the group asked.

Ammudien hoped to avoid revealing the shield out of fear that it would be taken from him, but he knew it was bound to come up. He opted to tell them some of the truth.

"No," he answered. "The elves returned the other pieces to the races who possessed them originally. With that said, I know where the shield of Sagrim is located, but no, I will not turn it over to the academy. None of you believed in the armor when I did. Therefore, the armor and the study of it will be solely my domain."

"You don't seem to be negotiating, but rather, setting terms. That's a bold move for someone who was practically ejected from the academy," cautioned one of Ammudien's former instructors.

"Perhaps, but it was I who found the armor, and it was I who first fought against the invaders. And I'm the only person here today who knows where the armor is. I'd say that puts me in a rather good position to make demands of those who once told me that I was a fool to believe in such 'fairytales'. And frankly, I don't think my demands are too great. I only ask to be left alone to continue my study of the armor and the magic that created it. Perhaps I'll be able to unlock the magic power in the shield that's been lost to us all these years and restore our abilities to their previous greatness."

The discussion went back and forth for several more minutes as everyone tried to convince Ammudien to accept concessions, including him turning over the armor to more 'experienced mages'. However, Ammudien stood strong against the opposition and maintained his terms and conditions. Ultimately, they agreed to Ammudien's terms. Their hesitation was less about their dislike or distrust of Ammudien and more about their unwillingness to admit they'd been wrong. Promoting Ammudien to the level of White Mage would be a very public and constant reminder of their mistakes.

Ammudien was allowed to keep the shield and was given free rein to research any subject he desired, but only as long as he shared his findings with the academy, which was one of Ammudien's own terms to begin with. A few days later, he was given his white robes in a private ceremony, another one of the council's conditions. This was followed by a public announcement that Ammudien was to be a lead researcher for the school. The announcement was needed to ensure that Ammudien was granted access to any and all of the materials inside the city's many libraries, both public and private.

Ammudien joyfully sent word to Nordahs in Rishdel of his new role and confirmed that the armor was safely in his care.

Nordahs could only laugh as he read Ammudien's note.

#

"I have a message for the king," the young boy said as he held up a scroll fresh from a messenger bird's foot.

"King Senna is busy acclimating to the needs of his new kingdom. He's not to be disturbed. You can leave the message with me," the king's second in command declared to the nervous lad.

"Yes, Lord Cooper," the boy stuttered before handing Rory the message.

Shortly after returning to Tyleco, Rory found himself summoned to Fielboro by Lord Senna. The summons didn't explain why his presence was needed, only that it was highly desired.

Upon his arrival in Fielboro, Rory Cooper, the former guard captain of Tyleco, found himself placed on the panel of judges responsible for determining the fates of those who were taken prisoner outside Brennan. And during the trials, Rory was seen as the voice of reason among so many voices of emotion.

Some on the panel voted for all of the prisoners to be put to immediate death by hanging. Rory countered those calls by saying that many of the prisoners were simply following the orders of their leaders, just as their own leaders would expect of them. Rory argued that it seemed unjust to put soldiers to death for no other reason than following orders and doing

the job they'd sworn to do.

"Had the situation been reversed, wouldn't you argue that you'd only

followed orders, and as such you shouldn't be treated as harshly?" he

asked the others to consider.

"The invaders thought we would be easy to conquer because our noble

sensibilities made us weak. While that assumption was proven wrong, I

think we owe it to ourselves and the people who look to us for guidance

and protection to demonstrate that we indeed are noble. Noble people do

not kill those who are undeserving. If we're to remain the noble people of

Corsallis and not become that which we just defeated, then we should

look to be noble in our judgments of others."

In the end, Rory's pleas spared the lives of many prisoners. Instead of a

hangman's noose, those spared were sent into exile, forced to leave

Corsallis together under the threat of death should they return. It was an

agreeable compromise.

Those who were identified as the leaders of the invasion force and directly under Shadrack's command were not so lucky.

And, of course, there was Draynard.

The crafty bandit made impassioned pleas to have his life spared. He vowed fealty to the new king, promised to give up his thieving ways, and assured the judges that he wouldn't interfere in any way. His pleas fell on deaf ears though, and it was unanimously decided that Draynard would hang with the others. The panel cited his willingness to betray his own race on the basis of empty promises of power, proving his utter untrustworthiness. Even the kind-hearted Rory voted to see Draynard hang from the neck until dead.

Rory's words and perspective during the trials had not gone unnoticed. The newly coronated King Senna felt that Rory's input would be very handy and helpful as he worked to rebuild the human towns impacted by the war. It had been a long time since a single monarch had power over all of the human towns, and King Senna recognized his own shortcomings when it came to understanding the inner workings and social customs of

the other communities. Rory's time as the guard captain of Tyleco gave

him insight into such things, and King Senna was eager to learn from him.

After the trials, King Senna approached Rory and offered him the title of

Lord, and a position as the king's advisor and personal guard. Rory jumped

at the chance and immediately sent for his family back in Tyleco.

It was a position fit for Rory, who promptly handed Raiken's sword to his

new king, who accepted it with grace.

"I will hold the sword as a sign of my right to rule," King Senna declared as

he accepted the sword from Rory. "But I think it is best in the hands of my

protector."

King Senna handed the sword back to Rory before using his own sword to

bestow Rory with a title, naming him Lord Rory Cooper, Grand Defender of

Corsallis.

And now, Rory had a message addressed to the king.

Lord Cooper took the scroll and carefully unrolled it. He'd determine if its contents were important enough to interrupt King Senna's other meetings.

The writing was rough and difficult to read at first. It looked like the writing of a child. Rory struggled to read the note, but eventually he was able to make out the rough writing.

'To the great and honorable King Senna.

Allow me to introduce myself. I am King Kelad[7] of Do'ricka. My father, King Pan, once called himself an ally of Macadre's former ruler, only to be betrayed when he refused to help with the failed invasion of your land. The fallen leader tried to assassinate my father after he refused to pledge our people to such a cause by having my father's ship sunk as he sailed home. Apparently, the dark one forgot that kobolds can swim.

My father returned to Do'ricka alive, but only just. He succumbed to his exhaustion soon after, but not before he told me what happened.

---

[7] Pronounced "Kel-lad"

Upon assuming my father's authority, I sought revenge by invading Macadre. When our forces arrived, we found only an empty city, devoid of any protection.

Rest assured that we acted mercifully and brought no harm to the city's residents unprovoked.

For now, the kobolds of Do'ricka hold Macadre under our rule, but we do not desire to stay here. It is our intent to return to our own lands and leave this land for your people. We will await word from you on who is to succeed our rule when we leave. I do not wish to leave the city and its inhabitants undefended or victims of thugs and thieves who may welcome such anarchy.

My father did do unscrupulous things in the name of my pack, thing I may not agree with, but I cannot change the past. I can only affect the future and look to grow our pack and our home through trade and alliances, not war and pillaging. I hope that our two peoples can learn to trust, and hopefully profit, from our bond.

I welcome trade with all races of Corsallis and encourage you to send word to your neighbors of our interests, but I start with you as a new king, like myself, looking to rebuild that which you care for most.

Kelad, King of Do'ricka.'

The note was most unexpected for Rory. The humans had very little contact with the people beyond Corsallis. The barbarians were the seafaring traders, but they'd never traveled to Do'ricka or had dealings with the kobolds.

Unexpected as it was, Rory didn't find the message of such critical importance as to warrant interrupting the king's meeting, so he opted to wait until the king returned.

When the king did return and Rory showed him the message, King Senna surprised Rory with his answer.

"Send a reply to King Kelad saying that we welcome trade and civility with the kobolds of Do'ricka. Invite him to meet with me here at Fielboro before his return to his home so that we may become better acquainted, especially if we're to work towards friendship between our people. And on the matter of who should rule Macadre, invite him to keep the city as an outpost here on our lands. Narsdin is a barren and forsaken place, but he and his people are welcome to whatever resources they find there, so long as they get along with the dark elves of Nectana. If he does not wish to establish an outpost alongside us, then I will find a suitable delegate to relieve him."

It was no small relief to Rory. He'd feared that his king would send him to establish order in the northernmost city, a place Rory had no real desire to visit, much less reside. The fact that King Senna offered to let the kobolds keep the city filled Rory with some relief. The kobolds would be fools to refuse such a generous offer. But the king's mention of sending a 'suitable delegate' removed any relief that had come before.

By Rory's face, King Senna could tell that his protector was fearful of receiving such an assignment.

"Fear not, Lord Cooper," King Senna started, "I would be a fool to send my senior advisor and personal guard to such a desolate place and so far from my side. Such an assignment would go to whatever groveler annoys me the most and who I trust will steal the least from me while there. I may be a new king, but I am not a foolish one."

The two men shared a chuckle at the king's final words before Rory left to have the king's reply sent to Macadre and King Kelad.

Over the coming weeks, the two groups grew more accustomed with one another. King Kelad agreed to retain rule over Macadre to solidify the relationship between the kobolds of Do'ricka and the races of Corsallis. The alliance would prove to be profitable to all, but best of all, it gave the kobolds access to new resources to help them fight the illness that still ravaged their island home of Do'ricka.

#

"I really miss Riorik and Wuffred. I wish I could talk to them again, especially Riorik. I can't help but feel I owe him an apology for what his family has gone through at the hands of our family," Nordahs said sadly as he looked up into the night sky.

A soft roar bellowed from beside the elf. Nordahs wasn't alone in the darkness of night. The great spirit Izu sat beside him.

Nordahs would talk to the bear, and the bear would growl and roar in response. Nordahs didn't know what Izu was saying, but deep down, he felt that his father's spirit was there and speaking to him through the bear. Nordahs made time to go into the forest once every fortnight to visit the great spirit. It was cathartic for the elf. He was able to say things in Izu's presence that he struggled to say to others. He unburdened himself about Riorik and Wuffred's death, the shame he felt for his father's actions, and the fears he harbored about not being up to the task of protecting the village. Izu always listened and replied in his bear-like way, and that somehow helped Nordahs to feel better.

In time, Izu and Nordahs could be found together during Nordahs' patrols and even on occasion walking through the dirt streets of the elven village.

On the few times that Nordahs had to leave the forest, Izu would always walk with him to the forest's edge and could always be found waiting for him when he returned.

Even his mother would sometimes sit and talk with the giant forest guardian. She often said she could sense Shadrack's spirit when she visited Izu.

Shadrack, the loving husband, father, and devoted Ranger, lived on through Izu, devoted to making amends for his own misdeeds by protecting others in the guise of the great forest spirit.

Epilogue

A few years had passed since Asbin gave birth to Wufrika. The baby had

now grown into a young child capable of running, playing, and talking, but

she was still years away from maturity, when magical abilities are usually

revealed.

The day started out much like any other. Wufrika loved to run around the

forge while Arala and Asbin worked on their latest masterpiece. The child, who was taller than most dwarves her age thanks to Wuffred's ancestry, could reach things that her mother and aunt didn't want to be reached. Fearful that the child would hurt herself, it was a constant struggle to keep Wufrika from playing with their tools and creations. For the most part, the pair did a good job of keeping the toddler out of danger, but kids will be kids.

Wufrika spied the handle of her mother's hammer dangling over the edge of a nearby table. Wanting to be like mommy, Wufrika decided to try and pick up the hammer.

The young half-breed with her bright red hair pulled out into pigtails made her way to the table. With her small hand, Wufrika stretched as high as she could to grip the bottom part of the hammer's handle. The young girl pulled and pulled at the tool, sliding it back little by little with each attempt.

Eventually, she managed to pull the hammer off of the table. The weight

of the hammer was too much for the young child. It slipped from Wufrika's

hand as it fell to the ground, landing directly on the top of her foot.

Wufrika immediately started wailing and crying in absolute pain.

Asbin came running inside to find her daughter crying hysterically and

flapping her arms up and down frantically. The former priestess was

brought to a standstill at the sight before her. What Asbin saw left her

stunned and frozen.

As Wufrika waved her arms about, Asbin could see runes being drawn by

the child's fingertips. All of Wufrika's fingers were creating runes. The

runes were incomplete, so they quickly fizzled, but it was an astonishing

sight all the same.

It was unheard of for a child of Wufrika's age to develop magical

attunement. It was equally unheard of for anyone to so casually create

runes with their fingers. A mage's wand was typically used as a focal point

to harness and channel a magical connection to create runes, but Wufrika
seemed to be able to do so without a wand's aid.

Asbin was confronted with the reality that her daughter was not only
magical but very magical.

But it was what happened next that sent chills down Asbin's spine.

She watched as her daughter stopped crying and opened her eyes. There
was an anger in Wufrika's eyes. The young girl looked at the hammer with
a hateful expression before picking it up with a single hand and hurling it
across the forge. The hammer smashed through the forge's wall and
became embedded in the stone of the nearby mountain.

Wufrika was also a berserker like her father.

##

Milton Keynes UK
Ingram Content Group UK Ltd.
UKHW021639260524
443160UK00001B/62

9 798350 72631